Acknowledgements

I'm going to keep this short and sweet. As always, first I would like to thank God for my talent and ability. I just want to say thank you to everyone that has believed in and supported my writing. Special shoutout to my readers group, ya'll fell in love with Sage and Zu first and encouraged me to explore this love story even further. Thank you to anyone who had a hand in pulling this story together and making it something special.

Foreword

This story is all about my belief that we don't live in a world full of fuck boys. It's an ode to the good guys out there that are loyal and sarcastic with a little bit of thug in them. The ones that appreciate a good woman when they see her and have the ability to lead with their hearts and not their dicks (all the time, anyway). This story is for the men that have their faults but can grasp the concept of communication well enough that they understand that problems are meant to be solved. The ones that take action when necessary, fall back when it's appropriate and cherish the beauty of a strong woman.

This love story is a tribute to all the people who still believe that a sense of fairy tale, *your own personal fairy tale,* still exists and that you're worthy of it. Love sucks sometimes; trust me I know. And it can hurt so bad that it affects your ability to be optimistic about its possibilities. But I still believe in it. I believe that happy endings aren't all the same and that most love ends up being a lesson that prepares you for the love of the right person. I also believe that one day I'll know the kind of love that I've written about and I'll trust that fact that I'm worthy enough to receive it. My hope is that this will encourage someone out there who is scared to love for fear of being hurt to look at things a little different and open themselves up to the possibility of loving and receiving love. Cuz love is dope.

Chapter One

Zuvhir

I watched her exit the store like a fuckin' creep. I didn't know her name, her age, her profession, or none of that shit. I just knew that she was *beautiful*. And that's some shit that I never normally call a chick. Fine, bad, sexy, lit...those were the words that left my mouth in regards to how good a female looked. But there wasn't another word in the English language to describe the woman that I'd let get away. I'd spotted her when she entered the store, and her presence sucked the air right out of my body. She was like a priceless work of art. Just looking at her made me feel something. A nigga like me had never wanted shit from a bitch except a nut, but something about her struck a different chord inside me, and it was weirding me out. Yet I was succumbing to it.

She'd entered the store, hurrying to get inside from the heavy rain, and as soon as she removed the snapback from her head, a nigga's heart started doing gymnastics. You ever felt your heart do back flips inside your chest? You ever felt that bitch stretch to capacity just looking at a mothafucka you didn't even know? You ever had to place your hand where your heart was just to keep it from escaping your body? Nigga, me either. Well, not until *today*. She did that to me.

Once she removed her hat, she shook her head, and her shoulder-length, jet black curls bounced on her shoulders, framing her oval face. Her skin was dotted with water droplets, causing her to sparkle under the gross, fluorescent grocery store lights. The cacao color of her skin was a stark contrast to my shortbread colored skin, but I could already see in my head that we would look good as fuck together. She complemented me. I just had to talk to her. But something about her aura had me stuck.

She was intimidating. And a nigga like me ain't never been intimidated by shit. But her? She had me frozen. So I just watched her. I watched as she maneuvered through the aisles of the store picking up fruits, browsing through the frozen foods, and lingering at the bakery. I watched her body move. And goddamn, what a body it was. She was nowhere near slim, but she wasn't close to being obese either. She was the perfect balance right there in the middle. She had thighs thicker than fish grease and an ass that was wide like her hips. It wasn't completely plump and high, but she had more than enough for a nigga to grab on. Even though she was dressed simply in ripped jeans and a v-neck white tee, I could see the pink lace bra that was pushing her large titties up and together, making her effortlessly sexy. Her shirt clung to her midsection, which wasn't flat, but it wasn't busting like a can a biscuits either. She was fuckin' perfect.

But she was intimidating. I watched her move from groceries to cleaning products and from the electronics section to houseware. But I still couldn't gather the nerve to approach her. Something about her had me hesitant. It wasn't a bad thing, but she was...she was *different*. Whereas I could usually pinpoint weakness and insecurities when looking at a female, I couldn't figure hers out. She carried herself like she knew that she wasn't perfect, but she was okay with it. She was confident in her flaws and even more confident in her attributes. She moved about like she had purpose...like she knew herself and dared anyone to challenge that. That shit had me shook a lil' bit. I was just a thug-ass nigga with tattoos and gold fronts. The streets was all I knew and fucking was the only thing I was really even good at. She made me feel like I couldn't offer her a damn thing but an orgasm and a headache. So instead of stepping to her, I just watched her exit the store like a fuckin' creep.

Chapter Two

Sage

"Why didn't he approach me?" I mumbled to myself once I was seated in my car.

I stuck the key in the ignition and let out a frustrated sigh. I'm sure that he thought I didn't see him, but I did. I saw him as soon as I entered the store. A chill shot down my spine at the sight of him, and it wasn't because of the cold rain that was pouring down outside. He was *everything*. From his light brown dreads, to his cocaine white teeth accented by a gold bottom grill, to the colorful tattoos that I saw peeking from underneath his Polo windbreaker. He. Was. Everything. He was the perfect height and weight, and when I caught him staring at my ass in the reflection of one of the freezer doors, I noticed that he had the perfect little dimple in his smooth brown skin. God couldn't have made a man more beautiful than him. He followed me around the store like a stalker, but he never attempted to approach me.

I looked down at the outfit I'd thrown on to run to the store. It wasn't some shit that I would wear to a fashion show, but it wasn't like I had walked out in pajamas and a bonnet either. And obviously, something about me had caught his attention or else he wouldn't have spent an hour bending corners just to get another look at me. I shook my head. I don't know why I was surprised. This was a typical thing. I could catch the eye of many, but it was rare that someone would actually approach me. The ones that did looked nothing like him, and I was forced to politely decline, which earned reactions ranging from "Nice meeting you anyway," to "Fuck you, bitch. You wasn't all that anyway." But I'd never been approached by someone as good-looking and perfect as him. And apparently, I never would. Sighing, I put my car in reverse, ready to go home and shake off my thoughts of him.

"*Fuck!*" I screamed before slamming on the brakes.

Good thing I had looked in the rearview mirror before stepping on the gas or I might have killed him. Rattled from almost committing second degree murder, I used my shaky hands to put the car back in park and hopped out. When I got around to my would-be victim, I paused. It was *him.*

"I...I'm so sorry. I didn't see you," I muttered, still taken by his presence.

"No need to apologize, Ma. I shouldn't have been standing there like a creep," he said, laughing and shaking his head.

"Like you shouldn't have been following me around the store like one?"

The question was meant to sound playful but the way that his head snapped up made me wonder if it had come off wrong.

"Damn, you noticed that?" He ran his hands over his freshly-lined dreads. "It wasn't like that. I...ain't a stalker or no shit like that. I was just...uh..."

I smirked as he tried with no avail to explain himself. For someone with such a thug appeal, he came off more shy than I had expected him to be. He seemed nervous to speak to me, barely looking me in the eyes. And I swear I saw his brown skin redden when I mentioned him following me. I couldn't stop staring at him. Although his swag screamed dope boy, I could see his soul was softer than his outward appearance. There was something melodic and gentle about him, and it made me want him even more than I did when I first saw him.

"What's your name?" I asked while he was still fumbling over his sentence.

"Zu."

"Zu?"

"It's short for Zuvhir."

"Zuvhir. Damn, that's kind of sexy." I'd meant to say that inside my head, but the sentence somehow made its way out of my mouth.

He smirked, finally looking me in the eyes. Damn, he was beautiful.

"Thanks, Ma. I just came to give you this."

He handed me my wallet that I never knew I'd dropped.

"Oh shit! I didn't even realize that I'd dropped it. Thank you so much!"

I reached out and grabbed the wallet from him, giving him a genuine smile. We stood there for a few moments, letting the now light rain continue to fall on us with no objections. I swallowed in his masculinity and attitude after I drunk in the sight of him for the umpteenth time. He was dressed in a pair of slim fit khaki pants, an army green Polo, and a matching windbreaker. His shoes were a pair of wheat Timbs. He filled out his clothes with his broad shoulders, and I could tell that he maintained an athletic body by the way that his shirt and pants clung to him. Thoughts of undressing him and exploring his crème brulee colored body, which I was positive tasted just as sweet as the aforementioned dessert, raced through my brain.

"A'ight, well you have a good one, Ma," he spoke, interrupting my dirty thoughts.

"Wait. What?"

He had already turned to leave, but he turned back toward me when he heard me practically yell at him.

"Huh?"

"That's all? You follow me around for an hour and almost died trying to give me my wallet, but you didn't even ask for my number? Hell, not even my name for that matter?"

"I'm sorry about all that in there. I—"

"I don't care about that," I said, cutting him off. "You're clearly interested in me, but you refuse to make a move. Why? You scared or something?"

I didn't understand him and it was making me angry. I knew for a fact that he liked what he saw, and for a man, I assumed he had more balls than he was showcasing. I couldn't wrap my head around the fact that he was playing me off. Even a nigga with a girlfriend or a wife would have gotten my number by now.

"Yeah," he replied simply.

"Yeah?"

"Yeah, Ma. I'm *scared*. Now just leave it alone. Have a good day."

He threw me a head nod and walked away. I watched him in awe, not sure of what had just happened or what he had just admitted. My heart stopped for the slightest of seconds as I witnessed him climb into his black G Wagon and skirt off. What the fuck?

Chapter Three
Zuvhir

Everything that I touched turned to shit. My life had seen so much tragedy that I was damn near immune to the shit. It was like a nigga was cursed. How can you explain a young nigga losing everyone that he loved by the age of 21? My momma, my sister, my grandma, my best friend, and the love of my life; they were all dead and gone. And in every instance, I felt like the shit was my fault. So when she asked me if I was scared, the honest answer was hell yeah. I was scared that she would just be another casualty. It wasn't just the fact that I couldn't get up the nerve to actually step to her, but I knew in the end she would be better off without me in her life.

But damn it if a nigga couldn't stop thinking about her pretty ass. She was imperfect, but she was perfect, you know? Like she wasn't a video vixen because she ain't have that type of body. But if I ever got my hands on her, I knew that she would fit under me like the missing puzzle piece. She was soulful. I could tell that by the way that she moved. I sensed that she wasn't excited by ordinary shit. Clothes, shoes, handbags, and trips would only excite her so much. She was the type that liked talking on the phone until four o'clock in the morning about nothing at all. I could tell that she liked poetry, wine, back massages, thunderstorms at night, slow kisses, and tight embraces. Those were moments that you couldn't capture in a picture, but you could explain in vivid detail by the memories it made. She was rooted and strong; a queen for sure. And from that one encounter, she had a nigga faded. She was intoxicating, and I didn't even know her name. *Damn.*

"Bye, Mr. Kingston!" I heard my students yell, snapping me out of my daze.

Doors slammed and lockers closed shut as I tried my damndest to shake off memories of the cutie from the store.

"KG, put your folders in your bag before your mom gets here!" I yelled at my little homie.

I was wrapping up my day at the student center, feeling bad that I hadn't really interacted with the kids like normal because ol' girl had been on my mind. Normally, I walked around and helped them with their homework or let them teach me a few of the new dance moves and shit. But I had just let them play freely today because my mind wouldn't rest. All the other kids had already left the center and went to wait for their rides outside except for KG and his little crush, Calaya. They had been drawing pictures of each other and laughing for the better part of an hour, but it was time for them to pack up and get gone so that I could dip too. I watched as they both packed up their backpacks, and I grabbed my snapback and headed toward the door to meet them.

"What ya'll doing this weekend?" I asked as I held the door open, letting the pair walk out.

"Me and my mommy going to Cedar Point!" KG exclaimed. "Do you like roller coasters, Mr. Kingston?"

"Yeah, man. Roller coasters are fun."

"Roller coasters are *scary*." Calaya frowned. "What if you fall?"

I laughed. "They have seatbelts and harnesses to make sure that doesn't happen. You ever been on one?"

She shook her head no.

"You should try it."

"I'll pass."

I laughed to myself. Kids were hilarious.

"Mr. Kingston!" someone call out.

I placed my hand across my forehead to block the setting sun and looked in the direction of the voice. That's when I saw KG's mom running around the back of her black Ford Explorer to meet us on the sidewalk. I always thought KG's mom was fine as fuck, but after seeing the girl from the grocery store, she seemed a little cookie cutter to me. Like I couldn't take away from her beauty. She was a dime. But to me she looked like every other Instagram model or reality chick. She had the whole small waist, big boob, tabletop ass thing going on and she had long curly hair. The Kylie Jenner lips were on deck as well as them long-ass butterfly lashes all the chicks were wearing. Ain't nothing wrong with none of that in my opinion. If chicks like it, I love it. KG's mom was smashable, no doubt, but the other chick had my head all fucked up.

"Hey, Mrs. Garrett," I addressed her once we were close enough.

"Go get in the car, KG. Calaya, your mom asked me to take you home, so get in with KG and buckle up, okay?"

"Yay!" the kids cheered as they ran over to the truck and hopped in.

"By the way, it's *Ms*, not Mrs.," she corrected me as she smiled flirtatiously.

"Okay, cool… What's going on? You need something?" I asked.

She tucked a strand of hair behind her ear. "Umm, yes…well….not exactly. It's more like I have a question."

I raised my eyebrow and waited for her to continue.

"Are you seeing anyone?"

I tried to stifle my laugh because I knew that shit was coming. All the mommas, single or not, had tried to get on a nigga since I had been working here. KG's mom had only shown her face once or twice, and when she did, she was always in a rush. So she hadn't tried her hand yet, but I should've known that it would only be a matter of time.

"I'm not. But I'm not looking to date either," I said bluntly.

"Really? Why?" Her smile was still wide.

"I'm just not in that head space right now."

She was silent for a moment, like she was trying to weigh her words. Finally, she nodded her head. "I understand that." She reached behind her and pulled a card out the back pocket of her tight-ass jeans. "If you ever find yourself in that head space, make me your first call." She handed me the card, winked and walked off.

I watched her hop inside her ride and I waved goodbye to the kids before I took a look at the card in my hand. It read: *Leigh Garrett, Branding & Marketing Consultant, 313-568-1147.* I shook my head before walking over to my car and hopping in. I tossed the card in my glove compartment and pulled out of the parking lot.

As I drove back to my crib, thoughts of grocery store shawty emerged. I tried to rid my mind of thoughts of her, but I couldn't shake her image from my brain. Everything about her had been emblazoned in my mind. She had consumed me, and I just knew I had to do something to shake her off. So I made a quick U-turn and headed to my nigga, Zeek's crib. I quickly switched from "Views from the 6", probably part of reason why I was so in my feelings now, to "Purple Reign" and headed over to the east side. Once I got there, I pulled up in his driveway and hopped out. I knocked on the door and Zeek's brother, Freak, opened the door and dapped me up.

"What up, nigga?"

"Shit, I can't call it. What you over here for?" Freak asked.

"Where yo' brother at?"

"Upstairs with Rena's hoe ass." He frowned.

I laughed. Freak couldn't stand Zeek's baby momma, and he never hid that fact. I didn't have a problem with her, but she was definitely a hoe fa sho and no one, not even her, could argue it. I never understood why Zeek even went after her. Yeah, she was good-looking or whatever, but her hoe fax was a few miles long before Zeek had even stepped to her. But shit, that was that nigga's life, not mine. So I just didn't speak on it.

"What ya'll got up later?" I asked, taking a seat on the couch.

Freak passed me the blunt he had just lit, and I took a pull. I exhaled the smoke and then took one more hit before handing it back to him. He ashed it out and then turned to me.

"Shit, I was probably 'bout to slide over to Eden for a minute to see what's poppin'."

"Yeah, that sounds like the move. I'm wit it. I need a distraction something serious," I muttered. "Ya'll straight over here with business and shit?"

Freak nodded. "Yeah, man, we good." He paused for a moment before looking at me and speaking again. "You know you more than welcome to hop back in position, my nigga. Yo ass gotta be bored by now."

I shook my head. A little over a year ago, I left the drug game alone. I had started when I was 17, and after losing all my people, I just ain't have the tenacity for it anymore. I had never been a real flashy nigga, so most of the money that I had made, I had stacked. I was sitting on a couple of mils, but I didn't have any clue what to do with it. Until I figured out what the hell I wanted to do with my life, I was just gon' chill. I had a little part-time gig at the student center because I liked being around kids and shit, but that was it. I couldn't lie and say that I didn't miss having something that consumed my day but, I didn't miss the risk and the loss you naturally took when you were dealing. So I was cool on getting back in the game.

"Nah, man. That's y'all's thing now. I just wanted to make sure Lupe was treating ya'll fair and shit after I stepped down. Trust me. If I wanted to be down again, ya'll would know."

After kicking the shit with Freak for a few minutes, I decided to leave, seeing that it was obvious that Zeek had got lost in the black hole that was Rena's pussy. I told Freak that I'd meet him and Zeek at Eden later and then I headed home. Once I got to the crib, I turned on ESPN and laid across the bed to get a quick nap in before the turn up.

Chapter Four
Sage

"When I tell you he was everything..." I paused dramatically. "He was *everything!*"

Butterflies attacked me at the same time an image of him popped into my head. There were not many men that you could classify as beautiful, but he was definitely one of them. I hadn't been able to get him out of my head since the grocery store. And I was still perplexed by his actions, so I decided to run it by my best friends, Hope and Reagan, in hopes that they would be able to explain what the hell had happened.

"Okay, so why aren't you talking to Mr. Everything instead of us right now?" Reagan sat down on the sofa with a glass of wine in her hand and her eyebrow raised.

"He told me he was scared," I admitted.

"He what?" Hope screeched.

"He said he was scared."

"So this tatted-up, swag daddy, semi god, bad boy, man-thug was scared of little ol' *you*?" Reagan placed her wine down and looked at me with wide eyes.

I shrugged. "That's what he said, girl. And then proceeded to walk away."

"Aww, hell nah! You ain't need his pussy-ass anyway! Talkin' 'bout he's scared! Of what? I mean, he followed you around like them chinks at the beauty supply store and then gon' come out his mouth to say he's scared? Boy, bye."

I cracked up laughing at Rae because she had no filter. She said whatever she felt and she didn't care who was around when she said it. Your momma, daddy, granddaddy, and your pastor could get it raw and unfiltered just like everyone else.

"See? That's exactly why we need to go out tonight and find us some real niggas," Hope stated as she clinked glasses with Reagan.

"When's the last time you found a real nigga at the club, Hope?" I asked.

I didn't know about her, but that was the last place I intended to find a man. The niggas in the club were mostly posers putting on a show with the money they needed to be paying child support with. The niggas in the club were paying over a grand in booths and bottles when they couldn't afford to buy a clue. They were out here announcing to the world via social media that they were about to shoot a movie in the club and would be struggling to put gas in their cars the following day. The last time I met a real nigga in the club was when Jeezy fell through in 2008. Fuck outta here.

"Don't be so literal. You know what I mean. I'm just saying we need to go out and have fun. Dance on a few laps. Let some guys buy us a few drinks. Give out a few fake numbers."

Rae and I laughed at Hope, but we were both game to go. I had been out of a relationship for a while, and I hadn't really dated in the meantime. I had been working so hard, trying to prove to myself that I could make it big without a degree that I had neglected the fun part of my life. I was overdue for some turn up. I called my cousin, India, the only relative that I had that still lived in Michigan, and invited her out. She accepted, and after wasting a little more time chit chatting, we all got up and proceeded to get dressed. I turned on Beyoncé's "Six Inch Heels" to get us in the mood, and we all went to work, beating our faces and laying our hair.

An hour later, we were headed out the door, each with a cup of pregame juice in our hands. Reagan looked bomb in a strappy black bandage jumpsuit with the sides cut out and a pair of multi-colored Steve Madden sandals. Her honey colored hair, which was all hers, was bone straight with a deep side part, and her only jewelry was a pair of large teardrop hoops. Reagan was slim with slight curves and long legs. She wasn't model thin, but she wasn't thick either. She stood 5'6" with butterscotch skin and pretty brown eyes.

Hope was a beautiful shade of chestnut with doe-shaped light brown eyes. In my opinion, she was perfectly proportioned with perky D-cup breasts, a small waistline, and a big African booty. She was wearing a silver body con

dress and a pair of neon yellow pumps with a matching
purse. She sported a jet black, shaggy bob with a wispy
bang, and her lips were painted with nude lipstick. A silver
choker and watch were her accessories for the night.

I had decided to go with a blush midi skirt and a tan
bustier top. My lightweight waist shaper had my body
looking right in the tight outfit, and it smoothed out my
problem areas; tucking in my stomach and pushing up my
ass. On my feet were a pair of Jessica Simpson nude patent
leather pumps and a thin gold choker sat around my neck
with a long gold bar necklace cascading from the bottom of
it. I carried a gold clutch and my lips were sparkling with a
light, glittery lip gloss. I had felt like straightening my hair,
but I just blow dried it and tossed it over one shoulder in a
long, messy fishtail braid.

Deciding to meet India at the club, we piled into
Hope's Jeep Commander and got lit while listening to a few
songs on my iPhone. The temperature was mild, which was
unusual for a summer night in Michigan, so we rode with
the windows down a bit to enjoy the night air. By the time
we had jammed to a mix of Beyoncé, Justin Bieber, Alessia
Cara, Desiigner, and Future, we'd made it downtown and

parked in the lot near Eden. I called India and had her meet us at the lot where we'd parked so that we could walk into the club together. India was an aspiring video model with a body to match the career she so badly wanted. She was dressed in next to nothing, which was not a surprise, but her face was beat and her hair was laid. People always told her that she looked a little like Lauren London, and I couldn't disagree. After bypassing the long line by paying the bouncer the VIP price, we strolled up the stairs and were escorted to the rooftop club.

The club was packed, but even through the throng of people, I spotted *him* right away. There was no one like him in the club, so my eyes automatically picked him out of the crowd. It was kismet, I was convinced. Chills raced down my spine once he turned and made eye contact with me. Our eyes locked, and I felt my soul dance. He smirked, but then he quickly replaced it with a frown. But I was unmoved. I knew that he wanted me. The combination of the light breeze that whipped around my body, the song that was playing, and the intense stare down we were engaged in made my body shiver with delight.

This thing we got is crazy, only thing I know is you're
my baby.
Forever down, I'm your lady. Always for sure, never a
maybe.
Never met someone who spoke my language
Never met a nigga done with playing
You the type of nigga make me lane switch
Hand me the brush and say 'paint it'
Give me your heart and I hold it, show me your soul
and I'll mold it.
Baby boy, you gotta be the dopest, gotta be to fuck
with the coldest
Boy you know all I do, is stay up all night losing sleep
over you
All I do, is drive myself crazy thinking 'bout my baby.

Kehlani continued to serenade the club patrons with a love song that matched perfectly with the way I was feeling. I watched him watch me intensely, and the feminine sensors in my body went haywire. The tension between us—even   though he was on the opposite side of the room—was stirring something deep down inside of me, threatening to bring me to orgasmic heights. He was touching me without touching me, and it was electrifying.

Fuck him being scared. There was something between us that was pulling us together, and I'd be damned if I left this club without at least his number. Tonight would be the last time he denied me of himself.

Chapter Five

Zuvhir

Fuck. In a sea of women, thotties, bitches, and hoes alike, *she* stood out like the North Star. She was guiding me home with her sultry brown eyes, but a nigga ain't wanna go. I was so conflicted. She was what I knew I needed, but I also knew that I was what she *didn't* need. She ain't need a nigga like me bringing all my bullshit and baggage into her life. She wanted a nigga, that much I knew, but I couldn't bring myself to fuck up her world like that. She needed to stay away from me.

But that was the opposite of what she decided to do. Obviously tired of staring me down from across the room, she and her bad-ass home girls made their way toward us, her eyes never diverting from mine. I watched her frame as it got closer and closer, and my mind drifted from thoughts of loving her to thoughts of fucking her. She made it over to us and poked me in the shoulder before placing her hands on her hips.

"Funny running into you here, Zuvhir."

The way my name fell from her pretty little lips caused my hands to ease over to the crotch of my jeans. Sheesh. Everything about her was making me harder than concrete. Before I could respond to her, she opened her mouth to speak again.

"Introduce us to your friends, Zu." She smiled, running her tongue ever so gently over her sparkly lips.

I laughed a little at her feistiness and turned slightly to my boys. "These are my niggas, Freak and Zeek. Ya'll this is..." I stopped short.

"Oh yeah, that's right. You ran so fast and furious from your future that you didn't get my name." She rolled her eyes. "This is Hope, Reagan, and my cousin, India."

I couldn't help but laugh at her snarkiness. She was really on one right now, talking about I had run from my *future*. I was right, though. She was confident in herself.

"That's your boo?" The chick that resembled New New from the movie, ATL, asked, eyeing me down like a piece of meat.

"Your future, huh?" I smirked, ignoring her friend. I wasn't trying to be rude but the only woman I could see was right in front of me so it didn't even feel right acknowledging someone else.

"Yeah, if you'd stop being so scared. I ain't the boogeyman, you know. Just a girl who wants to get to know you."

"You'd be better off if you didn't," I said honestly.

She cocked her head to the side and looked at me curiously. I knew that she didn't get it. Hell, I barely understood it my damn self, but I had this urge to protect her even if that meant protecting her from *me*.

"So, ya'll look like ya'll have some stuff to straighten out, so why don't ya'll buy us some drinks?" Hope looked at Freak and Zeek.

My boys agreed. Freak grabbed up Hope, and Zeek went for Reagan. India was the odd one out, and I could tell she felt some type of way. She smacked her lips and mumbled something about finding herself a sponsor before she strutted off in a different direction. Everyone else made their way to the bar while my nameless admirer and I stood there trying to figure each other out. She broke the silence.

"I don't even know why I'm asking because I know the answer. But do you like me?"

"Yeah, man. You cool." I shrugged.

She laughed sarcastically. "I'm cool," she repeated with an attitude.

Justin Bieber's "Company" blared through the speakers, and before I could protest, she grabbed my hand and led me to the dance floor. A nigga like me was more of a hold-the-wall type of dude while I watched a chick do her thing, but I was going to let her rock. She took complete control once we made our way to the middle of the dance floor. Pressing her body against mine, her back to me, she wrapped my hands around her waist and started to move to the beat.

Can we, we keep, keep each other company
Maybe we, can be, be each other's company
Oh company
Let's set each other's lonely nights
Be each other's paradise
Need a picture for my frame
Someone to share my ring
Tell me what you wanna drink
I tell you what I got in mind
Oh I don't know your name
But I feel like that's gonna change

It was crazy how a random-ass song could perfectly describe your mood as if you wrote it yourself. Justin was hitting the nail on the head with this one, and I couldn't help but fall under her sexy spell. The movement of her thick body against mine, the night sky painted with stars, and the light breeze made the shit seem like a love scene right out of a romantic drama. Without thought, I grabbed at her hips and turned her so that we were face to face. She looked up at me, her breath caught in her throat, and I wanted to lean down and kiss her so bad, but I resisted. Shoving her hands in my back pocket, she placed her head on my chest, whispering the words to the song.

It ain't about the complications
I'm all about the elevation
We can keep it goin' up
Oh, don't miss out on us
Just wanna have a conversation
Forget about the obligations
Maybe we can stay in touch
Oh that ain't doin' too much

This shit was too much. I reached out to push her away, but she wouldn't let go. Instead, she pulled me closer and swayed to the rhythm with more energy and intent. The chemistry between us was undeniable. We were attracted to each other like two magnets, and there seemed to be no force strong enough to pull us apart. I wanted her to steer clear of me, but my heart, for only the second time in my life, was overruling my head. I couldn't believe a nigga was drunk off this girl whose name I still didn't know.

The song ended, and she looked up at me with soft eyes, begging for me to say something. The internal struggle within was killing me. I wanted to give in, say fuck it, and throw caution to the wind. But I knew...*I fucking knew*, that I was no good for her. I knew that before we could become anything dope, I would fuck up things and hurt her. That was just my thing. And I was done hurting people. So I stepped back from her, causing a wave of hurt to wash over her face. She opened her mouth like she was going to speak, but instead, she just walked away.

I shook my head in disappointment. If I could be somebody else...if I could be a different nigga, a better nigga, I would be him for her. She was special. But it wasn't in me. So I watched her walk over to her girls, and my boys approached me.

"Fuck was that about?" Freak asked.

"I couldn't explain it if I tried."

Chapter Six

Sage

It was Saturday night and it was back to raining like cats and dogs. I stood on the back patio of my apartment, shielded from the rain, and watched it fall in large droplets to the ground. Something about the sound of rain was mystical to me, so any chance I had to enjoy it, I did so fully. Pulling the patio chair away from the wall, I took a seat and stared down at my phone. I'd been looking at it for hours, wondering if I should use it.

I had grabbed Zuvhir's phone from his back pocket during our dance and when I walked off, I dialed my number from his so I'd have it. After I saved my number in his phone and deleted the call, I gave it to his friend, Zeek, claiming that he'd dropped it. The tables had turned, and I had become the ultimate stalker. I'd never done no fatal attraction shit like that! But he had me open. I desperately wanted to know him and get inside his head. He was obviously battling his feelings for me, and I couldn't understand why. Everything in the universe was pushing us together, and whatever notion he had in his head was pulling us apart. There was something about him that I wasn't willing to give up on, so I had stolen his number. And now I was psyching myself out as I sat there wondering if I should call him.

I did okay with rejection. Sometimes shit just didn't go your way. But I wasn't sure that I could take another rejection from him. What if I called and he hung up on me? What if he made it crystal clear that I was not who he wanted? Oh God. What if another girl answered his phone? That thought was mortifying. But I couldn't help but feel like I would be missing out on life if I didn't take a leap of faith. He was supposed to be a part of me, my journey, and my soul, but he was fighting it. Well, I wasn't a quitter. *So here goes nothing*, I silently told myself. I opened up my contact list, selected his name, and placed the phone to my ear. My nerves shook like a stripper in church as I got down to the fifth ring.

"Hello?"

I let out a breath I didn't know I was holding. "Zuvhir?"

"Yeah, who dis?"

"Who did it say on your caller ID, fool?" I remarked smartly.

"How you gon' call my phone getting smart?" he laughed. "Who the fuck is Sage, yo?"

"Your future."

The line fell silent and I waited with baited breath for his response.

"What? How?"

"I used to be a bit of a klepto when I was in middle school, so it was nothing to pick your pocket on the dance floor."

"Damn, Ma. I'm going to have to watch myself around you, lil' five fingas."

We both busted out laughing and then returned to a comfortable silence. I knew that he was shocked, but I could also hear that he was lightweight excited that I'd called. I wasn't giving him room to doubt that.

"So what you doing, Zu?"

"Shit. Sitting here watching ESPN with all the windows and shit open. The breeze that comes in when it rains is crazy."

I closed my eyes, imagining being laid under his arms while the misty breeze swept through the room. It sounded perfect.

"Is that weird?" he asked when I didn't respond.

"Not at all," I said in a hushed tone.

"So what's up, man? I know yo big headed ass ain't call me to make small talk. What'chu want?" he asked playfully.

"I wanted to talk to you, duh nigga."

"Oooh, she got a little hood in her."

"Whatever. How has your weekend been so far?"

"It's been good. Nothing special. What you and your fly-ass girls been up to? Ya'll hang out last night?"

"Nah. Hope went to Atlanta to visit her family, and Reagan been cooped up with your boy. She's trying to be all secretive about it, but I am the Secret Service. I know things!"

He laughed, I loved the sound of it so I smiled wide when his laughter came through the phone.

"Damn, you all up in their business. Let them rock, Sherlock."

"I would if I had somebody to keep me occupied."

There it was. He knew like I knew that our conversation wouldn't carry on long without getting to the root of our obvious problem—*him.*

"Man, go on with that."

"Why do you keep fighting me? I know you ain't Stevie Wonder to the fact that we have chemistry. I know that you're feeling me, and you have me acting all out of my character trying to get you to give me a chance. Why won't you?"

"I like you, a'ight? But up until like 30 seconds ago, I didn't even know your name. How can I be feeling what I'm feeling for you and I don't even know you? Shit is wild."

"It happens. When your heart knows, it knows. You just gotta go with it."

"I ain't gotta go with shit!" he shouted. He took a deep breath before he continued. "I'm just not for you, man."

"How would you know that? You don't even know me," I argued.

"Because I do man! You...you...you're *different*. And you're special. You're like delicate and shit but tough at the same time. You got strong roots, but you ain't afraid to be wild and free. You got a life ahead of you. I can't mess that up."

The way that he'd just described me threw me off. It was beautiful and poetic, and I would have never guessed that's how he viewed me. If I wasn't intrigued before, I was now.

"How would you mess that up? You got a butt load of kids somewhere by different baby mommas? You got a crazy ex-girlfriend that's going to try and beat my ass if I come near you? You got problems keeping your hands to yourself?" I was getting frustrated, and it showed in my line of questioning.

"I got bodies, man," he said solemnly.

"*Bodies?*"

"Yeah, man, I said *bodies*...a collection of dead people that I loved with everything in me, gone because of *me*. My sister died because she rode with me to the store when I had niggas at my neck trying to take my mothafucking territory. My moms died of a broken heart because her only daughter was gone and she blamed me for that shit. My best friend got shot trying to protect me from a fight that was popping off. My girl died because I couldn't keep my dick to myself and my crazy-ass side piece sliced her ass."

I was stunned to silence. He wasn't lying when he said he had bodies. As tragic as it was, I knew it wasn't his fault. He must have felt the weight of the world, carrying around the pain of his loved ones' deaths on his shoulders. My heart broke for him.

"So I got bodies. No matter what I do, I always end up fucking up the lives of the people close to me. So I keep my distance. Yeah, I feel something for you, and it's strong as fuck. Hell, it might already be love, but I can't do that to someone else. I promised myself."

"It's not your fault, Zu," I mumbled, a single tear sliding down my face.

"I can't do it to you. So as much as I appreciate you checking for a nigga, I need you to lose this number and never call back."

"Zu! Zu! Zu?" I pulled my phone away from my ear and looked at it to see that he'd hung up. Fighting the urge to throw my phone off the patio in frustration, I walked back inside and slammed the door. I still didn't completely understand what was holding him back, but I understood more than I did before. He was broken. And he seemed not to want to heal. It was like he wanted to continue to bask in the pain of all of the damage he thought he'd caused. So maybe he was right. Maybe we were better off apart.

Chapter Seven
Zuvhir

It was 1 o'clock in the morning, and I was still up, laying on my bed, staring at the ceiling. Thunder crackled in the distance and a silent streak of lightning followed as I allowed my mind to drift. Off and on, my thoughts were filled with Sage. I was feeling her effort, but I just couldn't give in to it. A nigga like me was just better off alone in this world. I minded my business, stayed out the way, and fucked a few chicks here and there so a nigga wouldn't get backed up. But she wasn't a tossup. I could've dealt with just fucking her. But the way I felt when I was in her presence was different, and that alone made me steer clear of her. It was hard, and I felt bad as fuck for playing her off the way that I had, but she didn't understand. It was for her own good.

A knock at my front door followed by a series of doorbell chimes pulled me from my thoughts. I looked over at my phone again to make sure that I wasn't tripping. When the clock displayed 1:06 a.m., an irritated scowl took over my face. Hopping out of the bed, I grabbed my .45 from the nightstand and walked downstairs. I didn't have enemies after me since I was out the game, but a nigga could never be too sure. Unlocking the door, I swung it open to see Zeek standing there, his facial expression reflecting his irritation.

"What you doing over here?" I asked.

"Why don't you ask her?" he said, brushing past me.

Once he moved out of sight, Reagan and Sage appeared, and all I could do was shake my head. This girl was something else. Reagan offered a small smile as she passed me and entered the house and Sage just stood there, looking unsure.

"You came all the way over here to stand in the rain?" I asked her.

"Hell no, she didn't! Tell her to bring her ass in here since she wants to interrupt my night to come find you!" Zeek yelled from the living room.

Sage gently rolled her eyes and stepped inside, wiping her feet on the welcome mat. I closed the door behind her and watched as she took off her shoes and coat.

"You act like we were actually doing something, Zeek. We were just watching movies," Raegan replied.

"Yeah, but in 2.5 seconds a nigga was about to be 6 feet deep in that pussy until Fatal Attraction over here popped up." He rolled his eyes.

Raegan popped him upside his head and frowned. "Don't be calling my friend that! She just likes him. You losing pussy points with your attitude. Keep talking shit!"

"*Pussy points*? What the fuck is that shit, Rae?" he asked

"I got a system. You gotta make a score of 100 before you can stick your hand, tongue, or your little Oscar Mayer wiener near this thang." She patted her pussy through her pants. "You do good shit, you earn points. You piss me off, you lose points. Guess which one you doing?" She folded her arms across her chest and stared at Zeek.

I laughed to myself. She was a wild one. Probably just what Zeek's ass needed. Ready to get down to business with

Sage, I grabbed her hand and led her upstairs to my bedroom. After closing the door, I took a seat on the bed and motioned for her to join me. She did, and we sat in silence before she started to speak.

"Look, I know you probably think that I'm crazy. Hell, I'm starting to think that I am too. I've never gone this above and beyond to get a man because I damn sure don't have to."

I smiled at her confidence. I loved that shit.

"But you got me doing the most and I can't explain why. I feel connected to you and shit. Like if I was to let you go, if I was to actually let you walk out of my life like you want to, I would be missing something." She sighed as if she felt like she wasn't getting her point across. "Look, I can understand that you don't want to hurt me because of the things you've been through and I commend you for that. But you can't make that decision for me. If you are feeling me, which I know you are, you have to have enough faith in us that you're at least willing to try."

"How, man? How am I supposed to have faith when every time I've tried, I've lost? Every. Single. Fucking. Time. I don't want to just not hurt you. That's a big part of it. But I don't want to hurt myself either. I know that sounds selfish, but I don't care. A nigga couldn't survive that shit."

"Just let me be there for you. You need somebody, Zu. You can't go through life without somebody there to hold you down."

I watched as she moved from the bed and made it to where I was seated. She positioned herself between my open legs and just stared at me for a moment. A nigga started getting nervous and shit because I just knew she was about to do something I didn't want her to do, but my body didn't make a move to stop her. She lifted up the long dress she had on and she straddled my lap. Taking my face into her soft hands she lifted it up, forcing me to look into her eyes.

"I want to be your somebody, Zuvhir," she whispered.

My hands had a mind of their own as they moved toward her waist and stopped there. I held her firmly to keep her in place. Her body pressed against mine felt perfect, and I didn't want her to move an inch. Her fingers slid onto my scalp, between the spaces my dreads created, and I bit down on my lip. She was doing something to me, moving something inside of me and it was... Shit, I couldn't even explain it. She tugged on the bundle of dreads that she had gathered in her hand, and I squeezed her waist tighter. Her head fell back and a moan rolled off her lips so soft and delicate.

With her neck exposed, I felt like a vampire as I lunged forward and gently attacked it. I placed light, butterfly kisses along her exposed collarbone and trailed them up her neck, causing her grip on my hair to tighten. Easing her head back toward mine, she stared at me with lust swimming in her eyes. Thunder sounded off in the background, and a sudden wave of mist floated into the room through the open balcony doors. Sage shivered in my arms. Gingerly, she placed her lips on mine and just let them sit there as the wind, thunder and lightning intensified the moment. Unable to take it anymore, I grabbed at her nape and kissed her passionately. Goddamn, her lips were fluffy and soft like little chocolate marshmallows or some shit, and they tasted like it too. I found myself deepening the kisses, throwing my tongue in the mix and running my hands through the mess of curls on her head.

"Zuuuu…" she moaned.

I kissed her harder. She had said my name like its only purpose was to come from her mouth over and over and over again. The sound of it made my heart race and my body react. God help me. I had just done the last thing I wanted to do. I had fallen in love with this girl.

Chapter Eight

Sage

I hadn't felt this content in years and all I was doing was laying back and enjoying the soft, misty breeze that floated in and out of the open window. But I was wrapped up in *his* arms, and that made all the difference. We had found a comfortable silence and we were just marinating in it; each of us busy sorting through our thoughts. While nothing had been solidified, I hoped that my crazy behavior had convinced him that I wasn't going anywhere. I couldn't quite explain the connection I felt to him, but it had me acting out. I was acting crazier than crazy and I hoped that now, since it seemed like he had finally surrendered to my advances, some sort of normalcy and reciprocation would start.

"What you thinking 'bout?" Zuvhir held me tighter.

"'Bout how crazy I've been acting over you," I replied honestly.

"Yeah, man about that... I hope that shit is over because although I'm flattered by your persistence, I can't do crazy broads." He laughed lightly.

I smacked his forearm.

"I'm not crazy, boy. I just... I don't know. I saw something in you... a possibility... And it was something in me telling me not to let you ruin it. I always listen to my gut. It ain't never been wrong."

"Yeah, well you got me now so turn the nutty down a notch."

I smacked him again and we both laughed.

"You not going to keep calling me crazy, nigga. I..." I paused as what he'd just said replayed in my head. "Wait. So I got you now?"

Zuvhir was silent for a moment as he rubbed my now exposed thigh. I was laying between his legs with my back resting on his chest so I couldn't see his face. I wanted to turn around and ask him again, but I just waited it out.

"Yeah, you got me. I'm not saying we're official or anything. But I'm down with seeing where this can go. I don't want to move too fast."

"Move too fast? Boy, please. You love me already." I laughed jokingly.

When he didn't join me in laughter, I stopped and tilted my head so that I could see him.

"Would it be crazy if I did?" he asked, just above a whisper.

My heart started to beat so loud that I couldn't hear myself think. The thought of him loving me without even knowing me scared me half to death. I knew that there was something between us, but I didn't anticipate that it had grown to that level in a few days. I was excited at the possibility, but freaked out by the suddenness. I let out a low breath, trying to calm myself down before I answered his question.

"Yeah, a little. But it's been proven that crazy is a dynamic that works for us so I guess it's all good." I laughed a little.

"Guess you're right about that. You staying here tonight?" he asked.

I hadn't thought about it, but it was late as shit, and I was sure that Raegan and Zeek were probably knocked out by now. I didn't really want our night to end so I didn't mind staying. "Yeah, that's cool. As long as you don't try nothing."

"Girl, bye. I was about to tell you the same thing. Lil' freaky ass was straddling me like you was about to take the dick. Thought I was gon' have to call Olivia Benson on that ass."

The laughed that erupted from my mouth was loud and genuine. His laugh followed, and the crack of thunder was the only thing that caused us to stop.

"If you want to shower, the bathroom is over there. I'll get you some shorts and a t-shirt to sleep in." He tapped my leg, signaling for me to get up.

I got off the bed and he did the same. As he wandered into the hallway, I roamed around his room, looking at any and everything I could to absorb the essence of him. I looked at some family photos of who I assumed was his mom and sister and at the sports memorabilia that covered his shelves. I stopped short at a drawing that was partially hidden behind a large framed picture. Pulling it out from behind the frame, I picked it up and stared at it. It was powerful. My soul immediately stirred just looking at it.

It was an image of a man who had been shot. He was bleeding profusely as a crowd of people looked on. What was crazy about the picture was that the blood oozing from the man's chest was made up completely of words, written in red ink. Pain, broken, thug, stereotype were just some of the words that were repeated in the picture. I looked closer and realized that all of the people in the picture were also constructed from words. It was amazing.

"Damn, you a stalker and a snoop. We starting this thang off all wrong."

Zuvhir's voice caused me to jump. I turned toward him, slightly embarrassed that he had caught me lurking.

"Sorry. I was just looking at your photos and this was sticking out."

I looked at the picture again before looking back at him.

"Did you draw this?"

"Yeah, a long time ago." He walked up and snatched the picture from my hands and put it back where I'd found it. He handed me a fluffy brown towel and washcloth along with a pair of shorts and a t-shirt before heading back toward the door. "The shower is controlled by a keypad. It should be easy to figure out. I'm going to cook some food."

His attitude had shifted, and I immediately felt bad. Things were just starting to look up, and now I felt like I had done something wrong. Shit, I needed to just quit while I was ahead.

Chapter Nine
Zuvhir

What the fuck had I gotten myself into? Sage was a lil' baddie, no doubt, but I don't think I had fully realized what I had signed on for when I told her we could give this a shot. It meant that I was going to have to open up and let her in and it had been way too long since a nigga had done that, so I wasn't sure if I was cut for it anymore.

I shook my head as I stepped into the kitchen and headed toward the fridge. It was damn near four in the morning now and there wasn't shit open to deliver, so I was going to have to make do with what I had in the refrigerator. Pulling out some ground beef, onions, cheese and bacon, I got things together to make some burgers.

"You 'bout to whip, nigga?" Zeek said, walking up behind me.

"Yeah, I'm hungry as hell."

"Bet. Make me and shorty one of them joints too."

I nodded my head in response and got to cutting up the onions to go into my stuffed burgers. I placed the skillet on the eye of the stove and threw a few strips of bacon in the pan before going back to the chopping board.

"What's up with you and lil' mama?" Zeek asked.

"Hell if I know. She's cool, though."

"She's a good look for you. She's a lil' crazy, but you need a lil' crazy with your old-off-the-reserve ass."

I chuckled. He wasn't lying. A nigga like me kept to myself. I didn't party much and I stayed out the way. I damn sure didn't have my ass on none of that social media shit. It was rare that Zeek or Freak saw me after eight at night. A nigga was a homebody nowadays. I lived a boring-ass life.

"I don't know. I just don't want that shit—"

"Stop with that shit, man," Zeek cut me off. "You're fucking 26 years old acting like you're 75. You don't party or hang out. You ain't been in a relationship since Nadia. Nigga, you out here bad. Maybe Sage is what you need to shake shit up. You need to live a little. "

"Is that what you doing with Raegan?"

"He ain't doing shit but chillin' with Raegan. Bet that," Raegan answered as she sauntered into the kitchen.

"I knew you were crazy. Only crazy broads talk about themselves in the third person," Zeek retorted.

"Oh, I'm crazy now? I wasn't crazy when you had your nose pressed up against this pussy print. Stop frontin' for your boy, nigga." She mushed him and then took a seat on the opposite side of the breakfast bar.

"You gon' get enough of telling my business, girl."

"Never." She stuck her tongue out at Zeek. "Anyway, Zu, why you giving my girl such a hard time?"

"I'm not trying to. I just don't want to hurt the girl. I have a track record of that shit."

"Hmph. That's commendable, I guess. But Sage is persistent. If she really wants something, she doesn't give up easy."

"Yeah, I can see that." I laughed a little.

"Seriously, Zu. She likes you, and I haven't seen her act this way with anyone else. I know she's bringing you outside of your comfort zone, but give her a chance. Ya'll could be magic."

"Girl, shut the hell up sounding like a bargain basement romance novel." Zeek cracked up while Raegan slapped him across the back of his head.

"You shut up, dummy. Don't listen to him. Zeek could find magic too if his thirsty behind could think about anything other than getting his little eggplant wet."

Zeek rolled his eyes but didn't respond to that one. I smirked because I knew Zeek. He liked Rae a lot more than he was letting on, and I hoped that he would buck up and try to get to know her instead of hitting it and quitting it. As long as I had known Zeek, he hadn't been in a relationship;

just running through hoes like water, including his baby momma. But Raegan had potential. I planned on putting him up on game when I had a chance because she was a good look for him.

"What smells so good?" Sage's voice floated into the room.

I turned around and I couldn't help but smile at what I saw. Damn, she was beautiful. She had washed the makeup from her face, and her hair was piled up on top of her head in a mess. The hoop shorts I'd given her fit loosely on me, but they gripped her hips and thighs like a vice. She'd tied the big t-shirt I'd given her in the front, allowing some of her stomach to show. Sage blushed under my gaze, and I realized I had been staring way too long.

I knew in that moment that I didn't want another nigga to have a chance at what she was willing to give me. She was sacred and she had chosen me. That alone should have been cause enough for me to stop acting so damn scared and go with it. A nigga was still apprehensive, but women like her only came around once in a lifetime. I prayed to God that He wouldn't do me dirty and make this decision one I would come to regret.

Chapter Ten

Sage

I looked down at my phone and pressed the home button. No new notifications. I blew out a frustrated breath and turned the screen off. It had been almost a full week since I had spent the night at Zuvhir's house, and I had yet to see him again. We texted each other here and there, but he hadn't made any attempts to see me. I was trying to *dial back the crazy*, as he'd called it, so I hadn't made a move either, but I was getting antsy. I knew that this was a little new to him, so I wasn't upset with him. I was willing to teach him how to be in a relationship, but I just didn't want to come off...well, *crazy*.

I had half a mind to pop up at his house and force him to take me on a date, but I had already scared the man half to death with my aggressive pursuit of him. Now that I had him, I didn't want to run him away. So what was I supposed to do?

"Sage, do you have that clock-in report for me?" my boss, Amelia asked.

I hadn't even noticed her standing at my desk. My thoughts were too consumed with Zu to focus on much else. I worked as an executive assistant for a property management company and I liked my job more than most people working a 9 to 5 did. It wasn't what I wanted to do for the rest of my life, but it paid decently and my coworkers were pretty cool, so I didn't have any complaints for now. I eventually wanted to become a corporate interior designer, furnishing and decorating office buildings, hotels, and restaurants. But I had a long way to go before I could claim that as a career.

"Yes. I'll email it to you in just a second."

"Perfect. I also want to talk to you about something," she said, taking a seat on the edge of my desk.

Nerves started to get the best of me as I mentally ran through everything that she had asked me to do today. I was trying to figure out what I had done wrong. I didn't mess up often, but I didn't know what else she could want to talk to me about.

"Stop worrying." She laughed.

I breathed a sigh of relief.

"As you already know, we are opening a new condo development in Miami."

I nodded in response.

"Well, the property just passed inspection and we are about three weeks away from being able to put them on the market, but we have to set up the models so that our prospective buyers have something to view. I know that you and I have discussed your career goal of becoming a corporate interior designer and although this would be considered staging..."

"OMG! Yesss!" I screamed, cutting her off before she could get the rest of it out of her mouth.

Amelia laughed. "Before you say yes, let me give you the details. Accepting the offer to decorate the model means that you'll have to fly to Miami next Monday and you will have only a week to furnish and decorate the condo. The interior decorator that they hired is already decorating the other one, but I fought really hard for you to be able to do the second one."

I was bubbling over with excitement. This would be the first thing I would be able to add to my résumé, and it meant a lot that Amelia believed in me enough to trust me with such a big project.

"The condo is a 2,200 square feet with 3 bedrooms and 3 ½ bathrooms. Your assignment is to furnish and decorate the entire space. The company has given you a budget of $100,000, and like I said, the project must be completed in a week's time. Are you good with that?"

"I'm freaking *great* with that! Oh my God! Thank you so much. This means a lot, Amelia. Really."

Amelia grinned and nodded her head. Removing herself from my desk, she stood and straightened her skirt.

"You're very welcome. I will let the Miami staff know to expect you. You can make the travel arrangements. You don't have a budget for travel, so I would suggest that you pick a hotel that could serve as inspiration for your design. And book first class. Trust me. It's worth it." She chuckled.

My head was spinning with all the information she had just laid on me, and it was becoming hard to catch my breath. This was just the opportunity I had been waiting for, and I wouldn't let her down.

"I know that you're excited and probably need a minute to calm down so go ahead and take an hour lunch today. I have a late meeting anyway."

"Okay. Thank you again."

Amelia winked at me before she turned and walked back into her office. I quickly saved my work and clocked out for lunch, more than a little excited to call my friends, my cousin, and Zu to tell them the good news. Grabbing my phone and wallet, I made my way to the elevator. Once I reached the lobby, I paused for a moment, trying to calm down enough to figure out what I wanted to eat for lunch. I felt my phone vibrate in my hand and I looked down to see who the caller was. *Oh God.* There was only one person who could ruin my mood, and unfortunately for me, that's who was calling.

"What do you want?"

I was in no mood to deal with the drama I knew was coming my way from this unwanted phone call.

"Damn, that's how you answer the phone for your *fiancé?*"

Chapter Eleven
Zuvhir

Sage was heavy on my mind as I hopped in my truck and exited the parking lot of the student center. I hadn't seen her since we had chilled at my house and I was surprised that she hadn't popped her big-head ass back over here. I assumed she was trying to chill out, and I appreciated her listening to me, but I didn't expect her to fall all the way back. We had talked and texted in the meantime, and although I was happy as hell for her about the project her boss had secured for her in Miami next week, I felt myself getting a little sad about the fact that she was going to be gone for an entire week.

Since we hadn't had the chance to kick it with each other for real, I decided to change that tonight. Once I got home, I texted her to make sure she was free and asked her to swing by the crib at 8. I wasn't a romantic nigga by default, but I was going to give this thing a shot. She went out of her way to wear a nigga down, so I wanted to do something nice for her in return.

After I got out of the shower, I threw on a pair of black Robin's jeans, a white t-shirt, and a light grey button-down sweater. I slid into a pair of black Versace high tops and eased my silver Hublot watch onto my wrist. I pulled my freshly washed dreads up and secured them on top my head with an elastic band before spraying myself with Paco Rabanne's 1 Million cologne. Glancing at the clock, I saw that it was close to 8, so I headed downstairs to get ready for Sage's arrival.

As soon as I hit the bottom step, the doorbell rang. It was crazy. A nigga actually had butterflies at the thought of seeing Sage. That was some soft shit, but whatever… She was my lil' boo with her crazy ass. I smoothed down my sweater before approaching the door and swinging it open. A smile a mile wide formed on my face when I saw her. How was it possible for her to be even more beautiful than the last time I'd seen her?

Dressed casually as I requested, she was stunning. Sage was rocking a pair of ripped light wash shorts and a low-cut, baggy t-shirt with a strappy bra underneath. Her outfit was topped off with a shiny, light pink bomber jacket. She had them ugly-ass Creeper shoes on her feet, but somehow she had managed to make them look good. Her hair was pulled up in two curly buns, making her look hella young. She was perfect.

"Wow, you look nice."

She smiled as she stepped inside the house. I grabbed her up in a hug and pecked her on the lips. When I broke the embrace, she blushed.

"Somebody missed me, huh?"

"Don't flatter yourself, big head." I mushed her in the forehead.

"I know you're not talking with that watermelon resting on your shoulders."

I laughed as I turned around to grab the keys. Once I had them, I reached around her to hold the door open and motioned for her walk out, and she did. Once we were outside, I closed and locked the door. We hopped into my truck and sped away.

"So where are we going?" she asked as she searched for the AUX cord.

"Uh, lil' bit, what you think you doing?"

She looked at me in confusion. "I'm about the hook up the AUX cord."

"Nah, nah. Your lil' smooth jazz ass ain't 'bout to put me to sleep tonight. I only bump trap classics in this joint."

"Boy, bye. I don't even like jazz like that. I got you."

I shot her a skeptical look, but she just laughed and inserted the AUX cord into her phone. A few minutes later, Jon B's "They Don't Know" flowed through the speakers. I looked over at her, and she immediately burst out laughing.

"A'ight, girl. Keep playing with a nigga, and your AUX cord privileges are going to be revoked permanently."

"Okay, okay." She laughed.

She switched to some Gucci and I nodded my head. That was more like it. She already had me feeling soft as shit, so I needed something more hardcore to balance this shit out. The rest of the ride was relatively quiet with the exception of more trap music blasting along the way. I was surprised to see that she knew most of the words to the songs that played. She had me fully entertained as she rapped along to the songs. We pulled into the parking lot of the park, and I killed the engine.

"What is this place?" She looked around.

"It's called Top of the Park. It's kind of dope."

Top of the Park was pretty live. I had only been once in high school, but even then it was pretty cool. Taylor Park sat on top of a hilly part of downtown, and when you got to the top of the park, the view was crazy. So once a week, when the weather permitted, the city hosted this lil' event. Sometimes there would be a live band, and sometimes they would show a movie. People brought blankets and chairs and chilled out on the lawn. There were food trucks lining the entrance, and there was a few bars set up for the adults.

Tonight, they were doing spoken word, and it seemed like it might be something that Sage was interested in.

"Whoa, this is cool. I never knew about this place."

"C'mon."

We exited my truck and walked around for a little bit, trying to decide which food truck to stop at. I let Sage grab our food at the little burger joint while I headed over to the bar to grab us some drinks. The line was kind of long, so I found myself playing on my phone as I waited for my turn to order.

"This is a pretty romantic place for someone who's not trying to date." a female behind me whispered.

I turned around and came face to face with Leigh, KG's mom. I looked her over and couldn't help but notice how damn good she looked. Her thick thighs were wrapped up in a pair of short, multi-colored shorts, and her breasts were out in a black halter top. Her long hair was piled up on top of her head, exposing her slender neck and showing off her pretty face. She had on a pair of black thong sandals, showcasing her pedicured toes. There was no doubt that she was a fucking MILF. But unfortunately for her, a nigga wasn't even about that life right now.

"Ah, yeah... I guess you're right," I responded, unsure what to say.

"So I take it that you're on a date?" she pried.

I sighed. I hadn't exactly lied to her, but I felt just as bad about having to tell her about Sage. Leigh seemed like a cool chick.

"Yeah, man, I am."

"Interesting." She looked down at her feet. "So were you just not feeling me or—"

"Look, Leigh. You fine as fuck, Ma. It's just that there's this girl..."

"Is she beautiful?" she asked.

"Extremely."

"Is she smart?"

"Whip smart."

"Is she kind?"

"Definitely."

"Good. I'm not mad at that. You seem to deserve at least that much. If anything changes, you still have my card, right?"

I nodded. "I gotta warn you, though. I don't see shit changing with this one." I wanted to keep it as real as possible.

She looked at me, and I could see the disappointment take over her body language. Leigh attempted to grin and bear it, but I could tell she was a little let down.

"You're a good man, Mr. Kingston."

She took another look at me before walking away. I hated to hurt her feelings, but I flat out refused to hurt Sage's. I turned around to face the bar again and was surprised to see Sage there, holding our food in her hands. She smiled and stood on her tip toes to give me a gentle kiss on the lips.

"What was that for?" I asked when she pulled away.

"I heard your conversation with ol' girl. You at least deserve that. She was bad as fuck. I don't even think I would've turned that down."

We both laughed at that. This was why I couldn't disappoint this girl. She was perfect in every way possible. Any other chick would have tripped hard to even see me talking with another bitch, but Sage was so damn confident in herself that she could give a fuck less. Things like this made me fall harder and faster. Shit was crazy, man. Once we had our drinks, we found a spot near the front of the stage and took a seat.

"I have to say I'm pretty impressed with this. It's not where I thought you would take me on a first date," Sage said and shot me a smile.

"Where did you think a nigga was going to take you? The trap?"

She laughed. "No, fool. But I was thinking somewhere cliché like the movies or a restaurant. Definitely didn't figure you for a poetry in the park type of guy."

"This ain't something I do on the regular. I've only been once. But it seemed like something you might like."

"First up on the stage is a crowd favorite. He hasn't been to Top of the Park in some time because he's been busy making a name for himself. He's the dopest MC in the city and he's here to bless ya'll with a freestyle. Welcome Savage to the stage!"

As soon as the host introduced the first act, Sage started to choke on her burger. I looked at her with concern as she reached for the wine that sat next to her.

Damn, she's beautiful, skin like Hershey's
Attitude spicy, personality earthy
Humble but confident, I bet the bling on it
One of a kind, that's why I put a ring on it.

Dude looked in our direction with a crazy look in his eyes, and a nigga got real confused. I looked over at Sage and her eyes were wide as saucers. He continued to spit, and I looked between the two.

Had to dip for a minute, money was the motive
Baby girl hold it down, that's what I told her
Keep it tight for me mama, I'll make sure that rock gets bigga
Now I'm standing here looking at her on a date with anotha
nigga.

He looked directly at Sage this time. There was no mistaking that shit. Sage sat staring at him with a cloud of emotions hovering over her face.

"Sage, you better get to talking right the fuck now," I said calmly.

Chapter Twelve
Sage

He was such a fucking drama queen! I was having the perfect date and here comes this thirsty-ass nigga trying to make me look crazy. Not only was he looking at me with rage burning in his eyes, but Zu was looking at me like he wanted to murder me. And the audience was all in my grill because he'd put me on blast. Feeling overwhelmed and irritated, I hopped up from our spot on the lawn and walked away. Zu was right on my heels.

"I know you hear me talking to you, girl!" he screamed behind me.

I kept walking, not wanting to further embarrass myself by having a screaming match in the middle of the park. I felt a tug at my arm and I was whipped around so hard, I almost fell.

"Zu, that hurts!"

"Ask me if I give a fuck."

"Look, it's not what you think." I sighed.

"I wouldn't have to think shit if you had been upfront and honest with me. You running around here chasing me and this whole time you got a fucking fiancé?"

"No, I—"

"Yeah, that's fucking right."

I rolled my eyes when I heard Dominik's voice. He walked up on us, and Zuvhir's stance immediately turned defensive. Dominik smirked as he made his way over to me and draped his arm around my shoulder. I knocked it off and pushed him away, irritated that he'd had the audacity.

"Really, Sage? That's how we're playing it?"

"Yeah, nigga that's how we're playing it. I've been told you that what we had was over. I mailed you that gumball machine-ass ring back and I deleted you from every aspect of my life. What more do I have to do for you to get it?" I screamed in frustration.

"So this the nigga that's got you acting brand new?"

"Nigga, I'm right here. You want to know something, address me."

Dominik jumped up in Zuvhir's face, and I quickly stepped in between the two. I pushed Dominik in the chest, forcing him to take a few steps back.

"Dominik, stop it. Like, really... You know that it's a wrap between us."

"Stop playing with me, Sage. You know that we ain't never done. It's me and you 'til eternity."

Zuvhir laughed, causing me to turn and look at him. It wasn't an I-think-this- shit-is-comical laugh. It was more like a you-got-to-be-kidding-me laugh.

"Yo, I ain't beat for this shit." Zuvhir waved us off and headed toward his truck.

I ran after him, leaving Dominik where he stood, yelling my name over and over again like a broken record.

By the time I reached Zuvhir's truck, he had already gotten in and started the engine. I grabbed at the door, forcing it back open. Zuvhir looked at me, and my heart broke a little. He was obviously pissed and based on how Dominik had made things seem, he had every right to be.

"Zu, just let me explain. I promise it's not what he made it look like."

He remained silent, but his eyes moved a mile a minute searching me for something.

"Where's ya ring?"

"You heard me tell him I mailed it back to him. It's over between us."

"Yeah, well he doesn't seem to think so. I lay too low to be in the middle of some bullshit, Ma."

I sighed heavily. I was beyond frustrated. I had just gotten Zuvhir to see our potential, and Dominik just had to come and ruin it. "It's not like that! Dominik and I *were* engaged, yes. But I called things off when he up and moved to Atlanta to jumpstart his career as he claimed. I had to find out through Instagram that he had a whole family down there, and that was the real reason he left."

I could hear my voice getting shaky and I could feel tears beginning to creep. I had never hurt more than when I found out that the man that I thought I was going to spend the rest of my life with was tied to another bitch for the rest of his. He had a year-old son and another kid on the way. It was crazy because we had been together for five years. Even though I was over Dominik's cheating ass, it still hurt.

"He had a baby while we were in a relationship and he's got another one on the way by the same chick. I had no clue. I was playing house with a man that already had a home," I said sadly.

Zu's face softened, and he turned the car off. Climbing out, he pulled me into a hug and let me finish shedding the tears I so desperately wanted to avoid shedding. I hugged him back like he was my lifeline. I felt safe in his arms and that's the only place I wanted to be. I just hoped like hell he felt the same way.

"You got to dead that situation, Sagey. I'm a reckless-ass nigga when it comes to the people I love. It's obvious that he's not going to let you walk away easily, and I can't be in the middle of that shit. I will kill him, Ma. Bare hands. So you gotta straighten that out."

I heard everything that he'd said, but the only thing that stuck at the moment was the cute nickname he'd given me, Sagey. Without thought, I stood on my tip toes and planted a kiss on his juicy lips. He kissed me back, his hands moving from my waist to my ass, giving it a light squeeze. He broke the kiss and leaned back, laughing lightly.

"I'm dead-ass serious, lil bit. I'ma take you home, but until you are fully done with this situation with that lame nigga, I'm hitting the chill button."

I pouted, and he smacked my ass with force.

"Suck that lip back in. The quicker you make him understand, the faster we can get back to it. Now get your sexy ass in the car before you make me catch body in public."

I shook my head and pulled away from him to get in the passenger's seat.

"Got niggas writing poems about your ass and shit…"

Chapter Thirteen
Zuvhir

I could've handled that punk-ass nigga, Dominik, but Sage needed to handle him herself. Even though she claimed that she was through with him, I needed to be sure. And the only way I could be positive was if she cut all ties. Block his number, change hers, tell security at her building that he was not allowed past the gate; whatever she had to do to make sure that nigga got a clue, she would have to do before I entertained anything else with her.

After what happened with Natalie, I told myself I was done with drama when it came to relationships. I had actually told myself I was done with relationships period, but Sagey's little feisty ass had me going against my word. But the drama was a no go. That's how people ended up hurt. And fucking around with me, it was going to be how a pussy nigga got murked. So while she went to handle her situation, I decided to go and handle mine.

After I dropped Sage off, I hit up my lil' fuck buddy, Slice. Me and Slice had known each other since high school, and we eventually started running the streets together. She used to be a tomboy, dressing in baggy clothes and wearing a beanie on her head. But she was smart as fuck. So once we were out of high school, Slice went away to college and when she came back...nigga... She was a complete baddie. She had brown sugar skin, big doe eyes, and long, black hair that touched the small of her back. Underneath all of those clothes, she had a tight little body and she came back with hella tats in all different colors. She was the homie and she knew that our arrangement was strictly physical. I had tried to get at her as soon as she got home, but she made it clear that she wasn't interested in a nigga on that level.

I pulled in the guest parking space of her condo complex, put the truck in park, and hopped out. The door was unlocked for me, so I walked right in to see Slice sitting Indian style on her oversized sofa, rolling a blunt.

"What up, lil' nigga?" she asked before she wet the rello.

"Girl, please. You know it's not a damn thing 'bout me that can be classified as *little*."

"True. Ya mouth, ya ego, ya head..." She rolled her eyes.

"Don't forget about this pipe. If you forgot, I can remind you." I grabbed my dick for emphasis and she laughed.

I took a seat next to her on the couch and watched her seal the blunt. She was so damn pretty, but now that I had met Sagey, another chick's beauty couldn't compare— not even Slice's.

"Nigga, shouldn't you be down to your boxers already?" She lifted her eyes to look at me for a brief second.

Slice ain't play no games. Wasn't no drawn out conversation, no how was your day, no mental foreplay of any kind. We both knew why I was here, and there was no need to beat around the bush. Normally, I would have stripped before I came all the way into the living room, but I had a different agenda today.

"Yeah, but we need to talk right quick."

"*Talk?*" she asked like it was a foreign concept.

"Yeah, nigga… That other thing you do with your mouth and your tongue." I smirked.

She returned my smirk and lit the blunt before she flicked me off.

"Talk about what?"

"I met someone."

She looked at me curiously before blowing smoke out her mouth.

"*You?* You met someone?"

I laughed. "Yeah, man. Nothing solid so far, but I think she might be kinda special. I'm not trying to hurt her little crazy ass, so this'll probably be the last time I shoot through here."

Slice looked at me, and I could have sworn I saw sadness flash in her eyes. Maybe I was tripping and her eyes were just getting low because of the weed, but I decided not to read too much into it. She smiled between inhales and offered the blunt to me.

"Who would have ever thought?" She shook her head.

"I tried to get you on the team, but you wasn't having it," I joked.

"I know. I know." She ran her hands through her hair. "Silly me."

"Huh?"

"You a good catch, Zu. I know you don't believe it with all the shit you carrying with you, but you are. I was crazy not to give you a shot before, and ol' girl would be crazy to ever let you go."

"Don't tell me you getting all emotional over a nigga."

I shot her the side eye.

"Don't flatter yourself."

She cut her eyes at me and smiled, but the smile didn't reach her eyes. I wasn't sure what was going on with her, but the vibe in the room had just shifted. It almost had me rethinking about fucking her one last time. Before I could change my mind, though, Slice stood up and dropped her silk robe from her body. Her perky titties, flat stomach, freshly waxed kitty, and the barrage of tattoos covering her tight and toned body, immediately made my dick brick up in my pants. So much for changing my mind. Slice was definitely about to get this farewell dick.

Chapter Fourteen

Sage

I looked at the door for the twentieth time since I'd been here. I was anxious to get this over with because I missed Zu. Not only had we not seen each other since that night in the park, but he had been curving my ass to the left via text and phone for almost three damn days now. My phone calls went unanswered and the response to every text message was: *Did you handle that yet?* I was leaving for Miami in three days and the last thing I wanted to do was spend those three days without talking to my boo.

The truth was, I was scared as shit to face Dominik. He had hurt me so bad, and I knew that the pain he'd caused hadn't fully faded. But if I had to see him in person in order for Zuvhir to fuck with me again, so be it. I had watched Zu turn down a bad-ass female for me, so I'd be damned if I didn't show him that I was just as loyal as he was. I'd asked Dominik to meet me at a public place to prevent him from jumping stupid or trying anything. I just wanted to be done.

"Wassup, fiancée?"

I cringed when he called me that. Lifting my eyes from the coffee cup they'd been trained on, I looked right into Dominik's eyes. He was still handsome as ever with his golden brown skin, athletic body, and model like face. But he was a fuck boy in sheep's clothing. He took the seat across from me with a stupid smirk on his face.

"Stop calling me that." I grimaced.

"Why? That's who you are to me."

"No the fuck I'm not and that's why I'm here. You need to get it through your head that I'm done with you. I mailed you back your ring. I blocked you on social media. What else do I need to do in order for you to take the hint?"

"There is no *taking a hint*. When I put that ring on your finger, I meant forever. And forever is what's going down between us."

"This nigga is crazy," I mumbled to myself. "Look, forever isn't a part of the deal until we exchange vows and sign a marriage certificate. We didn't even get that far, so you can dead that."

"So you just going to throw away what we had for that nigga?"

I looked at him incredulously. I couldn't believe this fool was really acting like he wasn't the one with a whole family in another state. "Are you fucking kidding me? I didn't throw away anything! *You're* the one that went and had not one but *two* babies on me!" I yelled.

People in the small café turned around and looked at me, and I huffed in embarrassment. This was not going as well as I had hoped it would.

"Man, them kids ain't even mine. I got the paternity tests to prove it," he spoke as he stood to grab some paper out of his back pocket.

I stopped him. "It doesn't even matter. The damage is already done. *We* are done."

"Why you acting like this, huh? That lil' pretty boy got your head all fucked up, man."

"This lil' pretty boy will put some lead in you, fuck boy, so you better pipe down and keep me out of your conversation."

Dominik and I both jumped when Zuvhir's voice boomed behind us. I turned to look at him and I swear my pussy gushed. He was standing there being all thug and shit, and it turned me on in the worst way. His stance was defensive, but his face was eerily calm. I had never wanted to rape a nigga before. But looking at Zu in his black joggers, grey and red Bayside Jersey with no shirt underneath, and his dreads neatly twisted to the back, I was ready to catch a charge.

"Yo, why the fuck are you even here, bro?" Dominik's face was twisted with annoyance.

"I'm not your bro, nigga and I'd advise you to fall back. I may be pretty, but shit can turn ugly real quick," Zu growled.

I touched Zu's arm in an attempt to calm him down. People in the small coffee shop were starting to stare, and the last thing I needed was for a nosey white person to butt in or call the police. His body noticeably relaxed under my touch, and I took that as an opportunity to step in.

"I tried to be civilized about this shit after you completely disrespected me by having a whole family in Atlanta, but this is where I draw the line. We are *done*. I don't even have to tell you to stay off my phone, because a new number is in order since you can't comprehend simple things like a break up. Stay away from me."

"Bitch, you—"

Zu clocked Dominik so hard that he flew into the table behind him before he could get another word out. The people sitting around the coffee shop either shrieked or ran to try and help Dominik up. His nose was now crooked and bleeding profusely, but it served him right for all the shit he was talking.

"This ain't over!" Dominik yelled out.

"If you value your life it is, pussy nigga," Zu shot back.

I pulled Zu by his wrist out the door and into the parking lot before anyone could point him out to the cops. Too horny for words, I reached up and kissed Zu with all the passion and aggression my body would allow. I wasn't sure how he knew where I was, but that super hero, come-to-my-rescue shit he had just pulled, had me wetter than the Atlantic Ocean. After smacking me hard on the ass, he pulled away from the kiss with a smirk on his face.

"I will fuck around and kill that nigga over you," he remarked.

"I know, baby. But it won't come to that. I'm sure he gets the hint now." I eyed him down with lust.

"Girl, you better stop looking at me like you want me to bury something long and hard inside you."

"Mmm... Who says that's not exactly what I want you to do?" I asked before I bit down on my lip.

"I'm not fucking with you like that yet. If I think you crazy now, I ain't ready to see how you'll act once I bless you with this stroke game." Zuvhir ran his hands over his face, faking an exasperated sigh.

I punched him in the arm.

He laughed, "Chill, Ronda Rousey. Them little love taps actually kinda hurt."

I playfully flicked him off and turned around to walk toward my car. A few seconds later, he wrapped his arms around my waist, duck walking behind me. Zu nibbled on my neck as I squirmed trying to get away from him. He held me closer to his body, refusing to let me get away. Biting down on the skin in the crook of my neck, Zu caused me to inhale sharply and moan softly.

"Don't worry, Sagey. You'll get this dick soon enough. And when you do, I'ma bet that you won't want no other dick in your life as long as you live."

Chapter Fifteen
Zuvhir

"What you doing, Ma?" I could hear her adjusting herself on the other end.

"Nothing. I just got out of the shower and I'm about to throw some clothes in the washing machine. You?"

"Shit. Just came from hooping with my niggas. Tired as shit."

"You want me to come over and give you a massage?"

The thought sounded tempting, but I had to stay away from her for the time being. A nigga was already in love with her persistent ass, so there was no telling how gone a nigga would be once I slid up in her. So I opted to keep my distance, especially at night. My horniness be on muhfuckin' 100 as soon as the sun sets. I wanted to go about this differently with Sage, and that meant taking my time.

"Nah, Ma, I don't want you leaving out this late at night."

Sage sucked her teeth. "Boy, I'm grown."

"Yo grown ass ain't ready for this dick, though, and that's all you'll get if you come over here this late at night."

Sage sighed, and I knew she was about to get to whining.

"Zuuuuuuu, I don't understand. Are you not sexually attracted to me or something?"

"Fuck outta here with that shit, Sagey. That ain't even you. If I wasn't attracted to your sexy ass, we wouldn't have even made it this far."

"Then what is it?"

It was my turn to sigh. I knew that I had been playing it soft with Sage, but she had the uncanny ability to bring it out of a nigga. I had never been this wide open, not even with Natalie.

"Just trust me. We gon' get there."

Silence.

"So tell me something about you that I don't know. Something that makes you weird." I requested.

Sage giggled. "What the hell kind of question is that?"

"One I want you to answer. Now, c'mon."

I reached up and turned the TV down before propping myself up against my headboard as I waited for her to answer.

"Um, I can only fall asleep on a couch if music videos are on. And the volume has to be on 7. Anything else and I will toss and turn until I wake up and go get in a bed."

I paused before laughing.

"Yeah, that shit is hella weird."

"Shut up. Okay, now you gotta answer."

"I ain't weird, Ma. Next question—"

"Wait, wait, wait," Sage cut me off. "How you just gon' slide past my question like that?" She laughed.

"'Cuz this is about *you*. I'm trying to learn the most intimate aspects of you. I gotta know your soul and the measure of your heart..." I paused. "...before I can find out how deep in that pussy I can go."

I laughed and she joined me.

"See? You almost had me thinking you were a real romantic or some shit." She giggled.

"Nah, I'm just a mannish nigga trying to do right by the woman he loves."

Her laughter died down and she hesitated before she spoke.

"How do you know? How do you know that you love me, Zu?"

"You make me feel different. That's how I know. I've experienced another side of myself since you've been in my life. You make a nigga feel soft and shit."

Sage laughed and I smiled. I had never been this open before. And if I were being all the way real, it wasn't half bad.

"So what do you want to do...like in life?" I asked her.

"I want to be a corporate interior designer."

"Yo, you so weird. What kind of job is that?"

"It's not weird! Okay, imagine going into a casino that had no theme or a nice restaurant that had no décor to separate it from the hole-in-the-wall joints. Corporate designers turn businesses into art."

When she put it that way, I guess it made sense. I never knew that she had an interest in art like that. "Okay, okay. I got you. How did you figure you wanted to do that for a living?"

"When I was 16, I went on a HBCU tour with my high school. On our last night, we had this big fancy dinner at this expensive restaurant. As soon as I walked in, I was overwhelmed with the details of the place. Every little picture or wall trimming, glass, and plate added to the feel of the restaurant and made it magical." She paused. "I don't know. I just thought it was beautiful and I wanted to know how someone could have seen all of those things individually and realized they would go together perfectly."

"That's wassup. Art is dope. Any form."

"*Your* art is dope. How come you don't do it anymore?"

I took a deep breath. "I don't know. I guess I just couldn't really find the inspiration after my best friend died. I used art to express myself and to let out emotions that I couldn't put into words. But after I lost the last person that ever meant anything to me, it was like a nigga couldn't even feel anymore." I shrugged as if she could see me.

Losing my best friend had been the last straw for me. Nothing felt or looked the same to me anymore, and even though I tried to pick up a paint brush or a pencil, I could never put anything on canvas and paper. It was like I was empty.

"Well, I have faith that you'll find your inspiration again. Your artwork is powerful and it's worthy to be shared. Don't lose faith in your gift, okay? God gave it to you for a reason."

It was conversations like these that made me glad that I had stopped being so closed off. I wasn't the most religious person in the world, but I knew that God had sent Sagey to me for a reason. My only hope was that she was the one thing that I would get to keep.

Chapter Sixteen
Sage

"Let me get two of those end tables and that lamp," I requested, pointing out the things I wanted to the sales person at Z Gallerie.

It was my third day in Miami, and I had never had so much fun being alone. The new condos that my job had built were amazing, and I wasted no time sketching out a décor design and furnishing formation. On Monday, I didn't do anything but look through a slew of interior design magazines and binge watch a ton of HGTV, trying to construct a visual for the space I had been assigned. On Tuesday, once I had my plans laid out for each room, I looked up the best home décor stores in Miami and surrounding areas and planned out my day. I spent time looking at their items online and picking out the major things, like sofas and beds, to fit the design that I had come up with. I also browsed through Yelp and found the highest rated painting service and hired them to paint all the rooms in the condo. Then I went off to Lowes to buy paint. So today, the painters started painting and I was ready to do some real shopping. My first stop was Z Gallerie.

"Ok, what else, ma'am?" the friendly salesperson asked.

I had her follow me to the area where the dining room furniture was located. I stopped in front of a gorgeous, timber wood dining table that was flanked by regal purple velvet tufted chairs. The contrast between the earthy table and the luxurious chairs was perfect for the dining area although it was not the set I had initially picked out.

"OMG! Please tell me you have this table and eight chairs," I pleaded as I ran my hands along the soft fabric.

"I can double check. I'll be right back." She scurried away, probably happy as hell that her bright, sunny personality had attracted my attention when I entered the store.

Her commission from this sale was going to be pretty large. While she was gone, I took the time to call India to return a call I'd missed from her earlier. She picked up on the second ring.

"Hey, cuz, what's up?"

"Nothing. I was calling to see if you were over to Zuvhir's so that I could come grab the shoes that I left over there."

The Sunday before I left, we'd had a little dinner party at Zu's house. Rae, Zeek, Freak, Hope, and India had come over and we drank, ate, and played a few games. I don't know who told India to show up in a pair of gold Giuseppe Zanotti pumps, but she did. And by the time we were done with ghetto charades, her feet were killing her so she took them off. I had an extra pair of Jordan's in my car, so I let her wear those, but the heffa had forgotten her pumps at Zu's house. She'd texted me once I'd left Zu's and I hadn't had enough time to grab them from him the next morning before my flight.

"Girl, I'm still in Miami, remember?" I reminded her.

"Oh, shit. Damn, I wanted to wear them tonight, but I'll just wait until you get back."

"No, I'll text Zu and let him know that you're coming. You know his homebody ass don't ever go anywhere." I laughed.

"No, cuz. It's cool. I'll just wait."

"Girl, stop acting scary and just go get the shoes. I'm going to call him as soon as I get off the phone with you."

The girl that had been helping me on the floor came bouncing back up to me with a grin on her face.

"Okay, cool. I appreciate it, Sage. Love you!"

"Love you too, boo. Bye."

I hung up the phone and turned my attention towards the sales girl.

"We have the table and the chairs in stock. Well, we have 6 side chairs and two arm chairs. Is that okay?"

"That's *perfect*. I think that's all for the big stuff, but if you don't mind, I want to walk around and look at the décor and accents. If I see something I want, I'll come grab you."

She nodded her head excitedly and skipped off. I continued walking around the store as I dialed Zu.

"Sagey, baby, what it do?"

"Hey, baby. How are you?"

"Good other than the fact that I miss you. What you doing?"

I picked up a brushed gold centerpiece and flipped it over to check the price. "Picking out furniture. I swear I could do this for the rest of my life!"

Zuvhir laughed. "God willing, you will."

"True. Hey, babe, I was calling to tell you that India is on her way over to grab her shoes from the house."

I could hear Zu suck his teeth before he answered. "Damn, she couldn't wait until you got back?"

"I told her it was fine. She wanted to wear them tonight."

"A'ight, a'ight. You miss Daddy?" he asked.

I giggled. "Of course I do."

"Mmm hmm. Don't make me catch a flight."

"No, Zu. All you're going to do is distract me." I laughed.

"Fine, but don't be mad if a nigga can't keep his hands off of you when I see you."
"I won't be mad at all."

"A'ight, Sagey. I'ma let you go. Have fun, lil' bit."

"Thanks, Zu. Talk to you later."

I ended the called and just smiled at the blank screen like a dummy. Zu was *everything*. And although I missed him, I was glad that he wasn't here because I could guarantee that I wouldn't get any work done. I hit the home button on my phone and took a picture of the living room set that I was standing in front of. After I chose a filter, I posted it to my Instagram with the caption: Current job flew me to Miami to do my dream job. #luckygirl. After taking a quick Snapchat video and captioning it the same, I threw my phone inside my purse and got back to work. I still had $90,000 to spend.

Chapter Seventeen

Zuvhir

"I don't care how you slice it, Kevin Durant's decision to move to Golden State was *weak* in my opinion!"

The panel of sportscasters on TV erupted as a heated debate began. I picked up the remote and tried to find something else to watch because them niggas talking shit about Kevin Durant was starting to irk my nerves. Not that I was a huge fan of what he'd done, but the conversation was starting to bore the shit out of me. Before I could choose something else to watch, I heard the doorbell chime, letting me know that India was here. I grunted as I pushed myself off the couch and headed toward the door.

I wasn't a huge fan of Sage's cousin, but I never spoke on it because I didn't have anything to support my feelings about her. She never did anything out of the way, but I just got a weird vibe from her whenever she was around. Like when she came to the little dinner situation before Sage left. Knowing that everyone there was going to be booed up, she still came thru solo dolo. I appreciated her not bringing no outside nigga to my crib, but it was just weird to me that she would show at all knowing it was a couple's thing. But I don't know. Maybe I was just a weird-ass nigga. I walked to the door and opened it for a very wet India. I had to blink a few times to make sure what I was seeing was real, but after all that damn blinking, I still saw the same damn thing.

"Um, are you going to stare or are you going to let me in and give me a towel?" she asked, her voice full of attitude.

Without a word, I moved to the side so that she could come in and shut the door behind her. She was drenched in water from her forehead to her waist, making the white halter top cling dangerously to her big breasts, flashing her erect nipples. Lil' buddy in my hoop shorts started to stir, so I averted my eyes and jogged up the stairs to grab a towel for her. When I came back downstairs, she was topless, holding her titties in her hands.

"What the fuck?!" I yelled, tossing the towel at her and turning around.

"I was fucking cold, Zuvhir. You have the air on blast in here and the last thing I need to do is catch a cold," she snapped. "You act like you've never seen breasts before."

"Yo, chill with that." I walked over to the laundry room and grabbed a white tee out of the clean basket.

Before I could turn around to go give it to India, I felt her presence behind me as her breasts pressed up against my back. Her hands swiftly moved underneath my shirt, her fingertips caressing my six pack.

"India, man..." I shook my head.

"Don't tell me that you haven't thought about me since that night at the club."

I gripped her wrists and knocked them away from my body.

"I haven't. There is only one woman that has crossed my mind and she's in Miami."

Her hands drifted down my waist and to the crotch of my ball shorts, awakening the beast. I shook my head in frustration. Me and this nigga needed to get on the same page. I pulled away from India and spun around, which was the wrong fucking move. I was now facing her and could see her in all her naked glory. She had come out of her skirt, exposing me to the red lace thong that shielded her pussy from my view. Her fat lips were damn near swallowing the thin material and that only made my dick jump in excitement.

"India, you looking real thirsty right now." I brushed past her and out of the laundry room.

I could hear her following behind me and that only annoyed me. I kept moving until I got to the pile of clothes she had left behind.

"I don't care. I want you, Zuvhir, and I know you want me too. Sage don't know what to do with a man like you."

I made the mistake of pausing in disbelief, and India dropped to her knees in no time flat. Fumbling with my basketball shorts, we wrestled for control before I ultimately won out and pushed her back, causing her to land hard on her ass. After I tossed her clothes at her, I walked toward the front door and opened it.

"You're the type of bitch that I hate. You got everything going for yourself, but you're too busy comparing yourself to everyone else to see it. You so fuckin' insecure that you can't get up the courage to do the work of getting your own man. You gotta try and one up another chick by trying to take hers." I shook my head at her pitiful ass. "I'm not the one, sweetheart. Now get your shit and get the fuck out of my house!"

She stood to her feet, her face all tight and shit and slid into her skirt. I sighed. India was still taking her sweet ass time getting herself together, probably thinking I would change my mind. But she had no idea. Chicks like her made me even gladder that I had let Sagey convince me to open up. If this is what chicks were on nowadays, I didn't want any parts. This was the kind of bullshit that got Natalie killed, and I wasn't cut to make the same mistake twice, especially if that meant hurting someone as sweet as Sagey. She probably didn't know that her own cousin was plotting on her man, with her trifling ass. Ol' loose bitch... I was getting angry all over again.

"Hurry the fuck up!"

"Nigga, calm the fuck down. I'm going!" she snapped as she pulled the white tee I had given her over her head.

I had half a mind to ask her for that damn shirt back, but that would prolong her stay, all so that I could be petty. I wanted her out more than I wanted to embarrass her by having her walk to her car topless, so I let her live. She gathered her things and rushed toward the door.

She stopped at the threshold and turned toward me.

"I can promise you that little Miss Goody-Goody ain't going to put it on you like you're used to. So when you finally come to the realization that you need someone like *me*, I'll be waiting."

"Don't hold ya breath."

She stood there staring at me lustfully for a moment before I placed my hand on her back and pushed her onto the porch. After closing the door and locking it, I shook my head and adjusted myself. Now a nigga had to find some porn to watch or I was going to have blue balls in this bitch.

Chapter Eighteen
Sage

I inserted the key into the door and pushed on the handle. Walking into the hotel room, the air conditioner greeted me with a cool breeze. I was grateful to finally be able to relax. I had been gone all day, shopping for half the day and arranging and decorating for the other half. I was beyond exhausted and couldn't wait to lay across the king size bed and close my eyes. Before I could do that, though, I had to call my baby. I dropped my things on the dresser and ran to the bathroom to make sure that I didn't look a hot mess. After fluffing my curls and applying a little more lipstick, I took out my phone to FaceTime Zuvhir.

"Hey lil' bit."

I smiled as I watched his face appear on my phone. I could feel my soul brighten just from the sight of his smile. It was crazy that he had that kind of effect on me.

"Hey, boo. What you doing?"

"Sitting here staring at the wall damn near in tears because I wish my baby was home," he fake whined.

I laughed. "Aww, you miss me? Well, I miss you more."

"Impossible. So how did your day go?"

I watched as he adjusted himself so that he was comfortable on the couch. I wished so badly that I was laying across his lap with him playing in my hair.

"It was hectic. The painters painted one of the rooms the wrong color, so that set me back almost a half day. I think I have everything I need in order to finish the job, though, but I won't know until I finish with the stuff I already have." I sighed.

"That's good, Sagey. You enjoying it, though? Like, is it still what you want to do for your career?"

"Hell yeah! I think this opportunity had made me realize it even more. I'm in love with the possibility of doing this for the rest of my life."

"That's wassup."

Zu grinned, and I swooned because I could see that he was genuinely happy for me.

"You do anything today? Did India stop by to get her shoes?"

Zu's eyebrows knitted, and his lip curled up into a snarl. I knew beforehand that Zu didn't too much care for India. She was definitely an acquired taste, but most people warmed up to her sooner or later.

"Yeah. She came and got her shit," he responded tightly.

"You okay?" I asked. "Your whole demeanor just changed."

"I'm good."

Silence lingered in the air as I tried to figure out what the hell had just happened to cause our conversation to shift so drastically.

"Did something happen?" I finally asked.

"Nah. But look, I'm 'bout to meet up with Zeek and nem and grab a drink. I'll talk to you later. Love you."

"Uh... Love you—"

Before I could get the words out, my phone beeped letting me know that the FaceTime had ended. I stared at my phone in confusion. Not only was I confused about why he suddenly started acting so damn funky, but it was the first time he'd ever said I love you. I mean sure, he had told me that he loved me but we had never exchanged those words with each other. He hung up before I could tell him I felt the same way about him. I didn't know whether to be happy, frustrated, or irritated. I tapped my phone, poised to call him back, but I stopped myself. I was just going to give him his space. I refused to be one of those chicks that smothered a nigga.

Climbing out of the bed, I shed my clothes and hopped in the shower, anxious to wash the day off of me. After a hot and steamy 30 minute shower, I got out and dried myself off, spritzing my body down with Nude by Rihanna body spray. Once I was dressed in my short, silk night gown, I grabbed my laptop, my headphones, my eye mask, and my vibrator and got ready to get some much needed shut eye. I pulled up my iTunes and selected Tank's "Now or Never" album. Under my bookmarks, I found my favorite raunchy porn courtesy of XVideos and then made myself comfortable.

Get ready baby, this is about go down, go down
I know you got the word, that big daddy's in town,
town, town
I know you got your best songs for your boy
And I got some new hits you gonna enjoy, oh
Starting with your favorite song, girl we bout to get it
on
It's show time, I'm gonna hit the stage, girl I wanna get
you screaming

Something about Tank's voice made me horny beyond words. That nigga could sing the alphabet, and I'd be ready to cum off the rip. His voice coupled with images of Zuvhir in my head and the porn I had on mute, was definitely going to give me the orgasmic high I was looking for to put me to sleep. I got my vibrator in position and switched it on to its lowest setting. Small waves of pleasure prickled at my skin as all of my senses were overloaded.

"Mmmm," I moaned out loud.

We don't need no clothes for this,
They be on the floor for this
All up on the pole for this
Dropping down low for this
All up on the side with this
All between her thighs with this
Imagine how she ride with this
Wait til' I'm inside with this

"Sex Music" started playing, and that was my shit, so I upped the ante on my vibrator, switching it to the next highest setting. My eyes were closed at this point. I no longer needed the porn. I was imagining that Zu was there with me. That his tongue had replaced the vibrator between my thighs and that his strong hands were caressing my hips.

I imagined that my baby was the one that was turning my body into a smoldering flame that only he could extinguish. My body soon succumbed to my imagination. It felt so real that I could already feel my orgasm peaking just imagining that his tongue was doing all the work that my toy was at the moment. Arching my back off of the bed, sweat beads forming on my forehead, I released all of my sweet juices in an explosion of pleasure. My closed eyes tightened as I rode the waves of the aftershocks. It felt like he was there lapping up my sex like I was a melting cube of ice. When my breathing returned to normal, I finally opened my eyes, and the sight before me caused me to scream so loud I swear the maintenance workers in the basement heard me.

I wasn't imagining shit! But it wasn't Zuvhir. It was fucking *Dominik*. He stood at the foot of the bed with his face glistening with my juices. And he had a smirk plastered on his face. I had the sudden urge to throw up the sushi I'd eaten for dinner as I looked into his face. He unbuckled his pants and let them fall to the floor as he reached inside his boxers and stroked himself.

"What the fuck are you doing here! Get the fuck out!" I screamed as I scrambled to get off the bed and away from him.

"Damn, baby, you sure came for me like you missed me. Why you running now?"

He eased toward me, still stroking his dick. I panicked, looking around for something to defend myself. What the fuck was wrong with this nigga?

"How did you even get in here? How did you know I was here?"

"That was easy. Your Snapchat and Instagram told it all. As for getting your room key, all I had to do was show the front desk clerk our wedding invitations. She thought it was so sweet that I was trying to surprise my fiancée." He winked and nodded toward the large bouquet of flowers sitting on the dresser.

"Oh my God," I whispered. This nigga had lost his damn mind. "Dominik, you need to leave. I told you that we were over. And I meant it."

"You're lying. Did you see how hard you just came for me, baby? It was fucking beautiful. "

"I came for *Zu*! Not you, nigga!" I screamed, frustrated.

Dominik crossed the room in what seemed like one swift motion and clasped his hands around my neck. I could feel the balls of my feet lift from the plush carpet as my airway was being crushed by his tight grip. I clawed at his fingers while he silently stared at me, seemingly searching for something. I pleaded with him wordlessly as I felt my body weaken in his hands. *What was wrong with him?* He'd never done anything like this before. Tears sprang from my eyes, but I refused to be helpless. Taking what little strength I had left, I lifted my leg and drove it right between his, making hard contact with his exposed dick and balls. Instantly, I dropped like a sack of potatoes as he groaned and clutched his wounded member.

"Sage!" he screamed between groans.

But I was gone. I rushed out the hotel room with lightning speed. I bypassed the elevator, fearing that it would take too long to open and Dominik would catch up to me. Finding the doorway to the stairs, I burst through it and hurriedly ran down eight flights before landing at the lobby's entrance. I knew that I must have looked like a plum fool; hair everywhere, lingerie on, barefoot jogging through the lobby of an expensive hotel. I approached the counter and told the front desk clerk what had happened. Her facial expression transformed from confused to horrified to worried. She picked up the phone and called the hotel security to make sure that Dominik didn't leave the building and then called the police. Probably feeling bad for being the catalyst that set this whole thing in motion, the front desk clerk let me stay in the back office while she went to grab me a blanket and something for me to drink. While I waited, I used their office phone to call Zu.

"I don't want to talk about it, Sage," he answered immediately.

"I don't give a fuck about that!" I yelled, unable to control my emotions.

I was genuinely freaked out. Shit like that only happened in movies or network TV. To experience it firsthand had me shook. I couldn't believe that Dominik had become so hostile.

"Sage! What's wrong, yo?"

I had zoned out, not realizing that Zu was calling my name repeatedly. Before I could answer him, I burst into tears. "He was in my room. And he...he..." I tried to explain what had happened, but I was way too emotional.

"Who is *he*? Sagey, baby, calm down and tell me what happened. Matter of fact, fuck that. I'm on the next flight."

"Zu, no. That's not necessary. I'll—"

I heard a click on the other end and realized that Zu wasn't going to take no for an answer. I looked around the office for some Kleenex to wipe my face when a loud commotion made me peek my head outside the door. The police were dragging Dominik out in handcuffs, and he was not going quietly.

"It was a mistake! I didn't mean to hurt her! I swear!" Dominik caught me staring from behind the door, and he tried to break free of the officer's grasp to get to me. "I'm sorry, Sage. You were all I had left! She left me. Them not even my kids, man. I'm sorry. I'm sorry I hurt you!" he cried.

The police wrestled with him more forcefully and eventually led him out of the hotel. The front desk clerk came back with a blanket, cup of coffee, and a heartfelt apology. I nodded and waited as she arranged for another room to be cleaned for me. She explained that the room would be compensated as well as any food and beverage from the hotel restaurant. I knew that she was trying to make me feel better, but there was only one thing that would ease my nerves, and I wouldn't be able to calm down until I saw his face.

Chapter Nineteen
Zuvhir

"Oh my God, it feels so good to be home." Sage sighed as soon as she dropped her bags at the front entrance of her apartment.

I had met her in Miami that same night after catching the first flight available, not even caring that they didn't have a first class seat available. A nigga didn't like people all up my personal space, but from the sound of things, I didn't have time to waste. Sage needed me, and personal space wasn't going to be the reason I wasn't by her side. When I arrived at the Faena Hotel in South Beach, Sage greeted a nigga at the door, bum rushing me with a tight hug. As soon as our bodies collided, she broke down. Sage was such a strong person, so seeing her that distraught had me ready to wreck something.

She ran down the story of what that pussy-ass nigga, Dominik, had done, and I kid you not, I was ready to call in some favors just so I could get that nigga out of jail to personally put a bullet in his head. But Sage was able to talk me out of it, fearing that I would go to jail my damn self. She didn't know that I had law enforcement in my pocket still, but I decided not to physically harm that nigga myself for her sake. She had been through enough. She had filed a restraining order against him, and he had been arrested for sexual assault, so I knew that he wouldn't be much of a problem for us anymore. But for insurance purposes, I hit up my niggas on the inside to give him a message that I'm sure wouldn't be well received. But fuck that nigga.

"Baby, can you take my bags into my room? I'm going to whip us up something to eat real quick."

I nodded my head and grabbed her bags. Before leaving the room I placed a small kiss on her forehead. She giggled and bounced into the kitchen. I made my way to her bedroom and leaned her suitcases against the wall then took a seat on her bed. Zeek had hit me up about some drama with his baby moms and Rae and I hadn't had a chance to respond. As I pulled my phone out, I heard the front door open and close, but I didn't really pay it any mind. I was busy hitting Zeek with some real nigga advice. A few minutes into my text conversation, I heard a familiar voice. I stopped mid text, because I couldn't believe what the fuck I was hearing. Stuffing my phone in my pocket, I creeped into the hallway to hear the conversation better.

"I'm just saying that you need to keep an eye on that nigga. He legit tried to fuck me when I came to get my shoes, girl."

"Are you serious?" I heard Sage ask.

"Yes. I kept trying to tell that nigga that I'm not cut like that. Like, you're my fucking cousin! But he really tried it."

"I can't believe it."

"Believe it, honey. None of these niggas are shit. I hated to be the one to tell you about him, but I don't want to see my cousin out here being played. If he tried to get on me, I can only imagine what he doing with these other thot hoes."

"The same mothafucking thing I did with your schemin' ass." I said calmly, walking into view.

India jumped at the sound of my voice and her eyes narrowed once they landed on me. I couldn't believe the audacity of this broad.

"You ain't gotta lie to kick it, Zu." India said, mocking the line from Friday. "You know that you was all up on this acting like you wasn't already tied down by my cousin."

"Was that after you purposely ran into a sprinkler to make your shirt see-through? Or no, maybe that was after you stripped naked in my man's house and dropped to your knees to show him what your mouth do?"

Sage cocked her head to the side, waiting for India to answer her. India looked between me and Sage before Sage snapped her fingers to get her attention.

"Don't look at him! He's the last one that's going to throw you a lifeline."

I folded my arms and smirked, ready to see Sage go in on this desperate hoe.

"Sage, you don't know—"

"India, sweetheart, you are about ten seconds away from seeing me get real hood. I would prefer if my man not see that side of me yet, but I will not hesitate to throw these hands if one more lie comes out your mouth."

India huffed and folded her arms against her chest, causing her titties to spill out of her v-neck. *Look away nigga, look away.*

"So you really about to believe this nigga over your blood?"

I started for this scandalous bitch, but Sage put her hand up, motioning for me to chill. I relented. This is was cousin, so I would let her handle the shit.

"You know what's crazy? I almost did choose you over Zuvhir. When he first told me about you and what you did, I almost cussed him out for lying. I couldn't for the life of me understand why my own flesh and blood would cross me like that. Surely, he was just trying to cover his tracks after coming on to you."

Sage stepped closer to India, causing her to take a step back.

"Imagine how dumb I felt once he showed me the security footage from inside and outside his house. Imagine how painful it was to see my cousin be so determined to come between the best thing that has happened to me in years. Imagine how hurt I was to actually have to witness with my own eyes, the shit that people have been whispering about you behind your back all these years. And I almost lost him because I didn't trust him when really, I shouldn't have trusted you."

I shook my head at the conversation that was taking place. After Sage and I had handled the Dominik situation, she kept pressing the issue about India. She didn't understand why I kept avoiding her question about her visit and why my dislike for her had suddenly turned into hate. Over dinner, I tried to explain what happened but she wasn't trying to hear a nigga out. That fuck boy Dominick had done a number on her and understandably, she wasn't trying to trust a nigga. It wasn't until we got back to the hotel and I logged into my security system and showed her what happened, that she actually believed me. Even still, it had a nigga fucked up because she was letting the shit that other dude had done, affect how she handled me, and I wasn't with it. To be honest, even though we had hashed things out, it still bothered me that she didn't trust me. But that's another conversation for another day.

"Sage, I—"

Again, India tried to speak, but Sage cut her off, taking another step towards her.

"We are no longer friends. If I could do something about our lineage, I would because I damn sure don't consider you family anymore. Don't call my phone, don't acknowledge me when you see me on the streets and unfollow me on all social media. Wait, no. Keep following me bitch. I want you to have a daily reminder of the nigga that you couldn't get and how happy he is in the relationship with the girl who 'don't know what to do' with him."

Sage snatched India's purse from the breakfast bar and tossed it at her.

"Now get your trifiling ass out my face and out my house."

India caught the purse close to her chest and just stood there is disbelief. Not feeling her presence, I walked towards the door and opened it.

"You heard shorty. Get the fuck out, thirstbucket."

She opened her mouth like she was going to say something but then clamped it shut. She knew better. India kept her head down and exited Sage's place without another word. Once she was gone, I closed the door and turned around to face Sage. I pulled her body into mine and hugged her tight.

"I know that shit hurt, ma. But you did good."

"I'm sorry, Zu. I'm sorry I didn't believe you. I'm sorry that I didn't trust you."

I wanted to talk this shit out with her. In order for us to move forward, we were going to have to trust each other and even though she was apologetic about it now, I wasn't convinced that we weren't going to run up on this issue again. But I felt that she had had enough for one day, so I just held my baby a little tighter and decided to save that conversation for another day.

Chapter Twenty

Sage

"O-m-g, I can't believe that you said that!" Hope exclaimed as I finished telling her about my trifling cousin.

"Girl, I was about two seconds from lashing out. The only thing that kept me in place was the fact that Zu already thinks my ass is crazy. I didn't want to give him another reason to be looking at me funny." I chuckled.

"Well shit, he already know I'm missing a few screws. Let me have at that bitch."

"Calm your ass down, Street Fighter," Zeek said to Raegan as he entered the room. "We all know you're lethal with your hands."

"Yeah, you only know because I had to put your ratchet ass baby momma in the hospital. Stupid hoe." Rae rolled her eyes.

Hope and I giggled. We continued to talk as Freak and Zu came inside with the bbq from the grill. We were currently at Raegan's mom's house, having a little cookout. Rae's mom, Zena, was like a second mom to me and I had really wanted her to meet Zuvhir and give me her opinion. So far, she seemed to like him and I was glad.

"Damn, baby, that smells good!" Zena exclaimed in her raspy, deep voice.

Zena was a heavy smoker and although it did damage to her voice and lungs, it hadn't affected her outer appearance much. At 48, Zena put some of us young women to shame with her shape and long, pretty hair. Her teeth were a little stained and her lips were blacker than they should be, but she almost always had lipstick on to hide it.

"You know we some young grillmasters!" Freak said, popping his collar.

"Boy shut up. I saw you from the den. All your light bright ass did was stand there and run your mouth." Zena waved him off.

We all burst out laughing because we knew good and well that Zuvhir was the one who had put in all the work on the grill. Once Zu set the tray of burgers, ribs, chicken and hot links down, everyone started to move around the kitchen, grabbing plates and cups in preparation for our meal. I walked over to Zu and squeezed between him and the counter, brushing my ass against his lap on purpose.

"Don't fucking play with me, girl. You'll be the only thing I'll eat up out this mothafucka." He whispered in my ear, causing me to blush and giggle.

I knew he was just talking shit but any reference he made towards us being intimate always got me hot and bothered. I loved how mannish he was.

"You gon fix ya man a plate?" he asked.

"Yeah, I got you, baby." I smiled.

It had been a long time since I had been in a comfortable place like this and I was hoping that we weren't just in a honeymoon phase. Having companionship brightened my spirit and just overall made me happier. Knowing that I had someone dope to hold me down and support me, damn near had me feeling like I was walking on a cloud. I appreciated Zu more than he knew.

"Scratch that, Sagey. Can you go upstairs and get my phone out my jeans? I got hella barbecue sauce on my hands and a nigga ain't done drenching this meat."

"Haaaa! That's what she said!" Rae, Hope and I said at the same time.

We all laughed while the guys stood around shaking their heads.

"Ol' nasty ass little girls!" Zeek said, trying to hide his laughter.

"That wasn't what you was saying last night!" Rae cut her eyes at him.

"Nah, that's exactly what I was saying last night, witcho freaky ass."

Zeek rolled up on Raegan and pecked her lips before running away from the smack that she was about to hit him with.

"Aye! Watch your mouth in my house, boy! I don't want to hear about that shit you and my daughter be doing. Unless one of you got a fine ass uncle or daddy for me to do the same with."

"Ma!!" Raegan exclaimed.

I laughed to myself as I walked up the stairs and to the guest room where all our stuff was. The weather had played a little trick on us today and it had ended up being warmer than we had anticipated. The boys had come out of their jeans as soon as we'd gotten settled and now were just walking around in their hoop shorts and beaters. I found his jeans on the bed and fished his phone out of his back pocket. I must have accidentally hit the home button because his phone lit up as soon as I pulled it out. I looked down at it briefly, but what I saw made me take a closer look. He had several text messages from someone saved under the pizza emoji. And I know damn well Papa Johns, Little Ceasars and Domino's don't fucking text. He didn't have a lock code on his phone so, I swiped right to open it and went to look at the messages.

🍕 : Zuvy, way?

🍕 :I know what we talked about but I was wondering if you could fall through tonight.

🍕 : I need to see you. SHE needs to see you. 🐱

Oh, hell nah. This nigga thought that he was slick. My attitude immediately rose to ten as I stormed out the room and down the stairs. When I made it to the kitchen, I slammed his phone into his chest and attempted to brush past him, but he caught my arm.

"Yo, what's wrong with you?"

"I don't know. Why don't you ask that pepperoni pizza ass bitch that needs to see you?" I shot.

After a few seconds of silence, I looked up into his eyes, noticing that they had turned a darker shade of brown, almost black. That shit was scary. Zuvhir's normally neutral face was balled up in anger and I could see that his body had gone rigid.

"You went through my fucking phone."

"That's beside the point..."

He cut me off. "No, that *IS* the point."

Zuvhir dropped my arm and walked away from me, leaving me confused. How the hell had he turned the tables on me? I was the one that should be mad but now he had an attitude. And don't you know that nigga stayed mad for the rest of the night? What the entire fuck?

Chapter Twenty-One
Zuvhir

This shit was really killing me now. It had been two days since I had seen or talked to Sage and I was literally going *outside* of my mind. Normally Sage was over at my place after she got off work but I hadn't seen her since that shit went down at the party. Part of it was my fault. I had called myself putting her on punishment for doing some shit she had no business doing, but now I was just hurting myself. I wasn't in the business of hurting myself. As much as I wanted her to apologize for going through my shit, I knew there was a bigger issue that needed to be addressed and I was going to have to be the bigger person.

I had been running around all day, trying to get shit done for this surprise I had whipped up for Sagey and although a nigga was exhausted, I still had to get in the shower and get dressed. I had to go get my baby back. So as soon as I got in the house, I undressed and got in the shower. After 25 minutes under the hot, steamy water, I got out, dried off and lotioned up. Pulling my slightly wet dreads up into a bun on top of my head, I walked into my closet in search of something to wear. I decided on a pair of white,

destroyed jeans, a hunter green, short sleeve button down
shirt, and a pair of low top Balenciaga sneakers in the same
color. I pulled out a brand new white tee to wear
underneath and once I was dressed, I put on my silver Rolex
and a silver Cuban link chain. I took the dread bun down and
pulled half of it into a ponytail and let the other half hang
down. Once I was fully ready, I grabbed the bag I'd left at the
front door and went to go grab Sagey.

I pulled up to her place twenty minutes later and
hopped out my truck to go grab her. Just my luck, she was
coming out the house, dressed to fucking kill. She had on a
pair of ripped shorts showing off her thick, brown thighs
and a plain white v-neck shit. Over her shirt she wore a tan
vest that damn near reached her ankles and a pair of sandal
boot things that went over her knee. Her hair was wild and
curly; tossed haphazardly to the left side of her face. Got
damn she was beautiful. I missed her more now than I had
earlier. It was crazy. When she saw me, she stopped in her
tracks, looking me up and down.

"Fuck you 'bout to go?" I asked.

I hadn't meant to sound so heated but here I was barely functioning without her and she was carrying on like she was out here looking for my replacement.

"Excuse me?"

"You look good. Where you 'bout to go?" I said, softening my tone.

"What do you want Zuvhir?"

"Oh, now I'm Zuvhir?"
She just looked at me with a blank look on her face. I sighed.

"Look, I came here to talk to you. This shit has gone on too long."

"I don't want no explanation..."

I cut her off.

"I didn't come here to give you one."

Her head snapped up and she looked at me with wide eyes.

"What do you mean, you didn't come to give me one?'

Sighing heavily, I walked back to my truck and leaned against the hood. Sage stood there for a moment before deciding to walk towards me.

"I don't owe you an explanation."

"You know what? Bye."

She shook her head and started to walk away but I quickly lunged forward and snatched her arm. I pulled her close to my body and held her there, even though she was fighting to get out of my grip the entire time. I didn't care. I had missed her being close to me and I wasn't trying to hide that fact.

"Let me go, Zuvhir."

"No. You right where you need to be. Now calm your ass down and listen to me. And I mean really listen to me because once I'm done saying what I have to say, the conversation is dead and I should never have to have this talk with you again."

She leaned back and looked at me as if I had grown two heads. I didn't give not one fuck.

"I don't owe you an explanation because you didn't have the right to do what you did. You don't pay a nigga's phone bill nor have I given you a reason to not trust me so you going through my phone was a complete violation."

Sage started to interrupt so I bent down to kiss her lips.

"Every time you talk out of turn, I'm kissing your ass. And I know you mad at a nigga so if you don't want that, just keep your pretty little mouth closed til I'm finished."

Sage rolled her eyes.

"Now, as I was saying. You were in the wrong. This not trusting a nigga shit has got to go. I haven't done anything to make you think that I don't have your best interest at heart or that I would hurt you. I tried to save you from me to keep from hurting you. So now that I have you, why would you think I would jeopardize that?"

"I..."

I leaned in and kissed her lips, sucking on the bottom one before I pulled away.

"You asked a question!" she pouted.

Again, I leaned in and kissed her. Once I pulled away, she rolled her eyes so hard I thought them little suckers were going to turn into ping pong balls and bounce out. I laughed.

"It was rhetorical. But what I'm saying is that I would never be on no bullshit with you. Since you really want an explanation, I'll give you one. But it's not because I did something wrong. The girl that was texting me is someone I used to mess with before we got together. Just a friends with benefits type situation. When I told you to handle Dominick, I handled her. I haven't seen or talked to her since and don't have a desire to."

I could feel her body loosen in my arms. I smirked at her and shook my head.

"You gotta stop letting what that nigga did to you affect what we got going. I ain't him. I'm not going to do you like he did. I'll walk away before I hurt you Sagey. You ain't never gotta worry about that. But what I won't tolerate is you acting like a rat, going through my phone looking for something to be wrong."

"A rat?!"

I laughed before I leaned down and kissed her again. This time she surprised me by grabbing the back of my neck and pushing me deeper into the kiss. Snaking her tongue inside my mouth, she took control of the kiss and made me rock up immediately. I palmed her ass, squeezing a good handful of it before she finally pulled away.

"I got tired of you playing with me." She said and we laughed. "Am I free to talk now?"

"Yeah, go ahead."

"I'm sorry for going through your phone. The reason I haven't reached out is because I felt so stupid. I've never done anything like that before but I can admit that the situation with Dominik has fucked up my trust. I promise to work on it. Just be patient with me, please."

"You got it. Just try hard for me, ma."

Sage nodded.

"Now where the fuck was you 'bout to go looking like you about to rip somebody's runway?"

Sage giggled. "I was actually on my way to your house to see if we could talk this out. I missed you."

It was my turn to laugh as I pulled her closer to me. I kissed her forehead and then used her shoulders to push her back some.

"I thought a nigga was going to have to bribe you to talk to me so I bought you something."

"Oh, I should have held out a little longer." She joked.

I moved from the front of my truck to the passenger side, opening the door and grabbing the bag that I had for her. I walked back to Sage and handed it to her.

"Ooh, what is it? Diamonds? A Gucci bag? Some Christian Louboutin's?" she joked.

"Naw, but if that's what you want, I can get those for you too. Whatever will make you happy."

Silence fell between us as she pulled the large binder out of the bag and opened it. A small gasp flew from her lips as she realized what it was. I knew that with everything that had happened in Miami that Sage hadn't thought to do what I'd done so I did it for her. I had hired a photographer in Miami to take pictures of the work that she'd done at the condos and start a professional portfolio for her. Inside the large, black velvet and gold trimmed binder, were pictures of the entire condo that she had decorated along with matte black and gold business cards with her name on them. I had been working on this since the day we'd gotten back but I felt like now was the perfect time to gift her with it.

"Oh my God, no Zu. This is perfect. I didn't even think to...This..."

Instead of completing her sentence, she turned and wrapped me up in a hug. Making her happy was all that I wanted to do. There was no better feeling than to see the smile on her face knowing that I had been the one to put it there. I was glad that we had talked everything out and gotten clarification on our issues because that was how it was supposed to be. In a relationship you had to fucking communicate and that was the shit I had failed to do when I was with my ex. And I refused to make the same mistakes twice. Not when Sage's heart was at stake. Without realizing it, Sage had caused a nigga to man up and I was digging that shit.

Chapter Twenty-Two
Sage

"Heyyy, boo!" Hope waved at me from the other side of the restaurant.

I smiled and waved back as I walked in her direction. I joined her in the booth, sliding in and placing my purse on the opposite side of me.

"You look radiant, honey!" Hope exclaimed as she looked me over.

I blushed before reaching for the menu on the table.

"Thanks, love."

"Zuvhir must be blowing that back ouuuutttt!" she sang.

I threw a napkin at her as I looked around the restaurant to make sure nobody heard her loud ass.

"Actually, we've just been chilling."

"You a damn lie. You up in here glowing like you bathed in glitter and you talking about you ain't been getting no dick. Pssst."

I laughed. "I'm for real. We've just been getting to know each other and kicking it. No sex."

"Wow."

"I know. It's a first right? And it's not even me. He's been the one adamant about waiting."

"Girl, shut up." She looked at me in disbelief.

"Seriously."

"Well whatever he's doing is working, honey. I've never seen you this happy." She grinned.

I returned her smile and blushed, just thinking about how great Zuvhir had been to me. Hope was right. I had never been this happy and I was grateful to Zu for being the man that he was. Hope snapped her fingers in front of my face as I had drifted off into la-la land and we resumed our lunch. She talked my head off about Freak and their budding relationship, and I half listened because my mind was somewhere else. As the time continued to tick away, my nerves grew rapidly and Hope took notice.

"Hey!" she yelled to get my attention. "What is up with you?"

"Nothing...nothing..."

"No, it's *something* because you keep spacing out while I talk. Am I that damn boring?" She frowned.

I laughed.

"No, it's not that. I just have a doctor's appointment after this and you know how I feel about doctors and hospitals."

"Yeah, I do with your scary ass. What you going to the doctor for? A check-up?"

"No. I've been having really bad headaches lately and feeling nauseous. I've been sleeping a lot and having this weird tingling sensation in my legs, kinda like they are going numb."

"You sure you and Zu ain't having sex? Because that sounds like you're pregnant."

I shook my head profusely.

"Nope. Impossible. Look, don't listen to me. I'm just being paranoid. I'll be all right."

Hope looked at me cautiously.

"You sure?"

"Yeah, girl. Now finish telling me about how your cousin, Ronnie, and Freak almost came to blows."

Hope laughed before diving back into the story. I tried to pay attention, but deep down inside, I was worried. I was almost positive that this trip to the doctor's office wasn't going to end well.

Chapter Twenty-Three
Zuvhir

"Yo, they gon' wild out when they find out what we have planned." Freak laughed.

I chuckled to myself because he was right. Freak had been getting cool with Sage's home girl, Hope, and Zeek and Raegan were still going strong, so we decided to take them on a little getaway for a couple of days. It was high time we got out of this boring-ass city and see some other shit. I knew that the girls were going to be in for one hell of a surprise.

We had told them to dress casual for travel, but I knew they weren't thinking we were going on a road trip. Yeah, nigga... a *road trip*. True enough, we were breaded up and could have chosen to hop on a flight to anywhere we wanted, but touring random places with the homies was more adventurous, and we wanted to see if there was more than meets the eye with these girls. I knew that Sage was pretty down to earth, but Hope and Raegan definitely had some superficial tendencies according to Freak and Zeek. They were probably hella excited packing and shit, thinking that we were going to an exotic island or somewhere in Europe when really we would be stopping in little Podunk towns and tourist traps.

It had been two weeks since that incident with Sage and her old nigga, and we had been smooth. I had taken her off punishment and we had been kicking it on a regular basis. Either she would come chill at my crib after she got off work or I'd take her out somewhere. I had gotten to know her a lot better and I was right about everything that I had initially assumed about her. She was a perfect fit for me, and I wanted to make things official this weekend.

"Here they go."

Zeek pointed to Hope's car pulling up in the driveway alongside the rented Suburban. The girls hopped out the car, and I had to try hard as shit not to bust out laughing. Hope and Raegan were dressed like they just knew that they were going to run into paparazzi at the airport. Hope was wearing some tight-ass leather pants, a light knit sweater that fell off her shoulder, and a pair of sky high platform heels. Her shoulder-length hair cut looked as if she had just walked out of a salon and her makeup was done like she was about to do a photo shoot.

Raegan was a little more causal in a pair of high-waist black jeans, a baggy Van Halen concert t-shirt with a bunch of holes in it, and a pair of Christian Louboutin heels. Her hair was up in a smooth bun, and she had long bangs covering her eyes. Sage got out of the car last, and I smiled, glad that my lil' baby had followed my instructions. She was wearing a mustard body hugging t-shirt dress with a matching flannel around her waist and a pair of grey Chucks on her feet. Her usually curly hair was straight, and half of it was pulled up in a bun on top of her head. She didn't look like she had any makeup on, and her only jewelry was a pair of stud earrings. Looking at her dressed down like this made me want to give her the D real quick before we go on the road. I walked over to her and grabbed her bag, kissing her on the lips.

"Hey, bae." She smiled.

I swear my heart moved every time she showed me them pearly whites. A nigga had it bad for Sagey.

"What's up? Ya'll ready to roll?" I asked as I threw her bag in the back of the truck.

"Umm, can ya'll get ya'll asses over here and help with our bags?" Raegan shouted, full of attitude. "Swear, ya'll niggas ain't good for nothing!"

"Ain't nobody tell your dumb ass to pack all of Nordstrom's for a four-day trip, girl. The fuck ya'll got in these bags?" Zeek asked.

"Don't worry about what we got in them, rudeness. Just be a gentleman and get them out of the trunk," Hope shot.

Freak and Zeek walked over to the car and pulled the bags out with scowls on their faces.

"Yeah, a'ight, the joke gon' be on ya'll," Freak mumbled.

Hope reached up and smacked Freak on the back of his head.

"Say something smart again!" She frowned.

"Aye, this shit is a bad idea. I say we drop off Thing 1 and Thing 2 cuz I might catch a case fucking around with her violent ass," Freak said to me.

I just laughed because I knew he wasn't serious. We had planned this trip to a tee, and he liked her little feisty ass whether he would admit it or not. I popped Sage on the ass and told her to hop in the front seat since I was driving. Freak and Hope sat in the last row while Zeek and Raegan sat behind us. Five minutes later, we were on the interstate headed to our first destination. A half hour into the drive, we passed the exit for the airport and Raegan was the first to say something.

"Aye, you just missed the exit, Zu." She pointed out.

"Damn, did I?"

Zeek and Freak snickered as the girls looked around confused when they saw that I didn't try to turn back in the direction of the airport.

"Zu...," Sage started as she looked out of her window to see the passing airport.

"Surprise, nigga!" Zeek yelled. "Ya'll lil' bougie asses thought we were going island hopping, huh?"

"Thought you was about to be Snapchatting from Spain or some shit!" Freak laughed.

"Zuvhir, what the hell is going on?" Sage asked.

"We going on a road trip," I simply said.

"A *road trip*?" Raegan exclaimed. "Oh hell nah! Ya'll can turn this shit right around. Do I look like I do road trips?"

Zeek, Freak, and I burst out laughing. Sage punched me in the arm, and I swerved out of the lane a little bit.

"That shit ain't funny, nigga." Sage sounded angry, but I could see a grin tugging at her lips.

"Oh it ain't?"

"Hell naw that shit ain't funny. The hell are we going to do on a road trip? And a road trip to where? Where we finna sleep? I'm not staying nowhere that begins or ends with Motel. And I'm not about to piss in no gas station bathrooms!" Hope yelled from the back seat.

"Unless you gon' piss on yourself, then yes you are. Since you want to be all hoity toity about it, we can stop and get your grown ass some Depends then." Freak cracked up.

I looked in the rearview mirror and saw Hope and Raegan fuming and couldn't help but laugh too. I knew they would be pissed, but once they saw what we had planned, I knew they would loosen up. This shit was going to end up being kinda romantic if things went according to plan. Well, it would be as romantic as three thug-ass niggas could get. Sage had been practically begging a nigga to pipe her down since I fucked up her ex-fiancé, but I wanted to do something special for our first time, so I was holding out on her.

"So where is our first stop?" Sage asked, not looking up from her phone.

"Chi-Town."

Chapter Twenty-Four
Sage

Four long hours of bickering and smart comments was more than draining, but if I was being real, it was kind of fun. Once Raegan and Hope got over the initial shock of our actual destination, and Zeek and Freak got all their teasing out their system, Zu turned on some music and we vibed out. I made a Snapchat story about our little adventure, and we smashed some Carl Jr. burgers on the way. We only had to stop once for a bathroom and food break so we made good time getting to Chicago. We pulled up to the Renaissance Chicago Millennium Park Hotel, and I could hear Hope and Raegan breathe a sigh of relief. We filed out of the car while the guys helped with the bags.

"How long are we here for, bae?" I asked Zu over my shoulder.

"Just today. We'll leave in the morning."

"Well, we might as well hit the Miracle Mile while we're here! I hear Gucci and Saks calling my name!" Hope grinned excitedly.

"Uh, no, nigga. We ain't 'bout to be doing no damn shopping," Freak rolled his eyes.

"Yeah, ya'll brought enough shit to clothe all the homeless people in the state, so ya'll are for sure good on that."

"Sooo, what the hell are we supposed to do all day?"

"Chill, we got y'all covered," Zu stated and winked at me.

The guys grabbed our bags once the valet skirted off, and we went inside and checked into our rooms. Our room was beautiful and spacious with royal blue and yellow accents to accompany the stark white duvet and the tan furniture. I took time looking at the pictures and furniture accents, completely enthralled by how elegant yet modern everything look. I had almost gotten left in the lobby because I had been so busy staring at all its features. It was something that I wished that I had the pleasure of saying I had designed. I took a few pictures for my inspiration board and caught up with everyone else. Once we'd gotten settled in the room, Zu told me to shower and get dressed so that we could do whatever he had planned for us. Excited for whatever he had up his sleeve, I quickly showered and changed outfits.

I settled on a pair of ripped blue jeans, a long v-neck t-shirt and a gray suede cropped motorcycle jacket. I wore a pair of strappy gray sandals and I threw a pair of white chucks in my handbag just in case we had to get to walking. Zu got in the shower after me, and once I was done doing my hair and makeup he was done getting dressed. He was now wearing a pair of light wash Rock and Republic jeans, and a jean shirt in the same wash paired with a pair of blue and black patent leather Giuseppe sneakers. His dreads were in a sloppy bun at his nape, and a leather Halston snapback rested on top of his head. He looked damn good, and I honestly wouldn't have minded if stayed in the hotel ripping clothes off of one another. But for whatever reason, Zuvhir still wasn't having it.

"You look good, lil' baby." He smiled before he kissed me lightly on the lips, careful not to get my light pink lipstick on him.

"Thank you. So do you, boo. Where are we going?"

"Out." He smirked.

I rolled my eyes, and he laughed. Grabbing my purse, I followed him and exited the room. Once we made our way out of the hotel, we hopped in a luxury Uber.

"You mad that you're not yachting or island hopping like ya'll thought ya'll would be this weekend?" Zu asked once the car pulled away from the curb.

"Nah, not at all. The place isn't as important as the people you're with. So I'm good wherever."

"Uh huh, you say that now. But if we had pulled up at somebody's Motel 6 in Benton Harbor, your ass would've been hollering like Hope and Rae." He laughed.

I hit him in the chest and laughed with him. He was right about that. Motels were nowhere that I wanted to rest my head, but I trust that Zu wouldn't have put me in no weak-ass situation like that.

"Whatever. Ya'll be talking about us being bougie, but ya'll some ol' pinky lifting-ass niggas too. I'm sure that ya'll wouldn't have been trying to lay your head in some roach motel."

Zuvhir chuckled and shook his head. "Nah, you right about that."

A few minutes later, the car stopped, and Zu hopped out to open my door. We were in front of a place called The Chopping Block, and Zu was wearing a huge grin on his face.

"Remember you told me that you could cook better than me?" He asked and I nodded my head. "I ain't made you show me ya skills yet, but today you 'bout to show Daddy what you working with."

He pointed toward the window, and that's when I noticed the "Couple's Cooking Class" sign. I smiled wide and bright because he had been listening. I had told him on numerous occasions that the only other job I would have wanted in life would have been to be a chef. I liked to hunt down complicated recipes and try my hand whenever I had the free time, so his decision to bring me to a cooking class was perfect.

"You think you're cute, huh?" I poked him in his left dimple.

"Nah, I *know* I am." He laughed.

We walked into the restaurant and were greeted by the hostess. She handed us aprons, and I made a quick Snapchat video of Zuvhir looking all fine with his thug ass after he put his white apron on. While we waited for the instructor, I sent a group chat to Rae and Hope and told them where we were. Hope replied back first, stating that Freak had taken her to some place called Robot City where you could build your own robot and compete in a small competition. I thought that was so cute because it was right up Hope's alley. She was a mechanical engineer, so anything that involved her using her brain and her hands to construct something was dope to her.

Raegan responded shortly after stating that we were boring little grandma's because she and Zeek's wild asses were about to take a helicopter tour of the city. Before they took flight, they were getting piloting lessons and they would each get a turn to pilot the helicopter. Rae's little dare devil ass was too geeked. The boys had really put some thought into this trip, and I was thoroughly impressed.

"Everyone ready? Tonight's menu consists of prosciutto wrapped grilled shrimp, sautéed beef tenderloin with blue cheese butter, and oven roasted beans with almonds. And for dessert we will prepare lemon and whipping cream tartlets."

The instructor, who was a small, middle-aged white lady with short curly hair, clapped her hands together and immediately started teaching us how to prepare the meal. She was bubbly and full of jokes. I'd never had so much fun cooking in my life. Zu had a lot to do with it because he kept stealing food off of my chopping board, trying to juggle and taste more than he was cooking. I was in awe of him because he was so loose and carefree and I had never seen him act that way before. He was affectionate, kissing my cheek or nibbling on my neck every chance that he got. And he was talkative too, asking the instructor questions and requesting that I Snap everything. I didn't know what had gotten into him, but this other side of him that he was showing me, made me fall hard and fast. I knew what I was getting into when I pursued him as hard as I did, but what I hadn't expected was to have to hand over my whole heart so quickly. But he hadn't even asked, yet here I was ready to lay it right at his feet.

Chapter Twenty-Five
Zuvhir

I, low-key, didn't expect to have as much fun as I did cooking and shit, but Sage brought out the kid in me. I was so relaxed around her, not worried about shit other than her enjoying herself. That was new to me. But I was feeling it and I was feeling *her*. I had never really been the type to go out of my way for a chick, but Sage had me planning and listening like a lil' white boy in a romance flick. Like now, Sage had been complaining about having a headache since we left the restaurant, so I sent her to the lobby to go get some aspirin while I had a masseuse table set up in the room.

The hotel had tried to sell me on their spa package and shit but wasn't no other nigga or female for that matter, gon' rub up on my girl. So I just had them bring the table, the oils, and some candles to the room, and I would do the rest. I set everything up while Sage was downstairs so by the time she came back, the lights would be off and the candles lit. The massage table had been placed in the middle of the room and a candlelit milk bath had been drawn courtesy of the hotel staff. I didn't know nothing about that shit, I just shoved the spa lady a handful of bills and told her to make it happen. When I sent Sage downstairs to get the meds, I made sure that the lady at the front desk talked her head off about the décor to allow us more time to prepare. When she finally made it back, shit was perfect.

"Oh my God! Zu! What is this?" Her hands flew to her mouth as she took in the room.

I laughed at her reaction. "I wanted to help you relax. Go in the bathroom and slip in the tub. I'll be out here when you're finished."

I grabbed her hands and placed them on my chest as I leaned forward and kissed her pretty lips. When she pulled away, I nodded my head in the direction of the door and she walked away to get settled in the bathroom. Once she was inside, I grabbed a few blunts from my bag and went out on the balcony to smoke. As soon as I opened the patio doors, the crisp wind blew in and threatened to wipe out the flames inside the candles so I quickly closed the doors behind me. Sparking up, I pulled my phone out and saw that Slice had called me. I stared at the phone in confusion, wondering why after I had ended things with her, she was still hitting my line. Curious, I dialed her back.

"Zu," she answered.

"Wassup, Slice? Everything good?"

"Yeah, everything's good."

Silence lingered on the line while I tried to figure out if she was going to tell me why she had called or if she was going to play games.

"What'd you call for?" I asked, tired of waiting for her to speak up.

"I...I...uh...I just wanted to hear your voice."

I chuckled. "Ok, then. Now you heard it. Is that all?"

Slice huffed. "Really, Zu? Now you're going to be an asshole since we're not dealing with each other?"

"I've always been an asshole, sweetheart. But what's really good? I'm confused as hell as to why you hit me after I told you we couldn't kick it no more."

"I just—"

"Nah, Ma. Give me the truth or get off my line."

"You want the truth? The truth is I miss your ass, ok? And before you start going in on me, I know that you said you were with someone else, and I'm not trying to mess with that. I don't think. I just... I don't know."

"Man..."

This was the shit that I wasn't trying to hear. Slice had ample time to get at a nigga even though I would have turned her down for fear of hurting her ass. Now that a nigga was unavailable, she wanted to push up. I refused to hurt Sage like that. Shit like death and accidents I couldn't control. But *my actions*, I had complete control over that, and Slice wasn't going to be the reason I experienced or caused more hurt.

"Zuvhir, look, I didn't think I had feelings for you like that until I felt the void from being without you. I know this seems sorta left field, but I just had to say something to see if there was a chance. You know me. I'm not a home wrecker, but I'm also not one to hold my tongue."

"You're right. You're not a home wrecker. You can only be one if I allow you to be, and that's the shit I won't do. I don't ever want there to be any animosity between us, but if you can't fall back and be a friend, we need to leave this shit where it stands and go our separate ways. I promised that girl I would protect her from me and I will honor that promise no matter what friendships fall by the wayside. You cool, Slice, but I'm not losing her for shit."

Another round of silence settled between us. I was just about to hang up when she finally spoke.

"You love her?" she whispered.

"Crazy as it sounds, I do."

"Ok," She responded, sounding defeated. "Take care, Zuvhir."

"You too, Slice."

I hung up the phone and slipped it into my pocket, sighing deeply. I cared a lot for Slice. She was the homie, but I didn't do drama, and I refused to let this relationship end like my last. I sparked up the L again and smoked on the balcony until two blunts were gone. Good and high, I walked back into the hotel room and removed my shirt and jeans, and pulled on some hoop shorts. I decided to stay bare chested because I knew I was about to get lotion and oil everywhere. A few minutes later, Sage came out of the bathroom dressed in just a fluffy white robe.

"That was amazing." She grinned.

"You ain't seen nothing yet." I motioned toward the massage table. "Hop up."

Shyly, she untied her robe and then hesitated to let it drop to the floor.

I walked over to her and grabbed her hands, removing them from the place where she held the robe closed. "Don't do that."

"I know you've seen my body in clothes and that's all well and good but it's another thing entirely to see me without the help of shapers and pushup bras. I don't look like these video girls on Instagram. Everything ain't neatly tucked and raised and I just...I just don't want you to be disappointed." She sighed, lowering her head.

The woman who was normally so damn confident was appearing before me more naked than she could ever be, yet I couldn't see one stitch of her body. She was vulnerable and she was even more perfect to me now that I could see that she had flaws. I picked her chin up with my finger.

"You think I give a damn about a little stomach action or some thighs meeting in the middle? I love you, Sagey. So I love every inch of you."

I opened her robe and pushed it over her shoulders, keeping eye contact with her the whole time. Finally, when I could feel her confidence coming back, I let my eyes roam her body. Once I was done with the front, I took her hand and spun her around, her light giggle was music to my ears.

"I love them big ol' chocolate brown nipples and I love each little dimple in that big ol' booty. I love every zebra stripe on your hips and every pound that sits on your stomach. There isn't anything to be embarrassed about, lil' baby."

She tried to hide the smile that was building, but it broke the surface and spread across her face like wildfire.

I smacked her ass hard. "Now go get up on that table so I can take care of you."

Before she walked away, she grabbed my face and kissed me passionately. She let me know how much she appreciated my words with the way she worked her lips on mine and then she went and climbed up on the massage table. The shit I had said to her wasn't for show. It was real as fuck. I didn't love Sage because she was a carbon copy of what society told us to like. Yeah, I liked a flat stomach and perky titties just like the next nigga, but I was more than happy with the way that Sage looked, so she didn't need to be ashamed of shit.

For the next hour, I massaged all the kinks out of Sage's body. I went from her pretty little toes, to her toned calves, to her thick and chunky thighs, to her wide, meaty ass. I paused when I got there, making sure to kiss all over that mothafucka because it looked good enough to eat. I continued up her back, took care of both arms and worked my way up to her shoulders and neck. By the time a nigga was finished, Sage was ready to tap out. It was all good, though. I had no plans to sex her tonight. This was all in preparation for what was to come. The day I put this dick in her life, there was no turning back, and I had to make sure she was ready for that.

Chapter Twenty-Six

Sage

It was our second day on the road trip, and we were apparently headed to St. Louis, Missouri. It wasn't my ideal place for a vacation, but it was somewhere I had never visited before, so I was down to explore. Zu had done such a dope job with our first stop that I felt the need to repay him. I begged for like an hour straight to get him to let me plan our day in St. Louis, and after a few small arguments, I won out. He was curious how I was going to top his outing when I only had a few hours to plan it, but I was competitive and up for the challenge. He told Zeek and Freak that I was planning our day and the boys ended up requesting that Hope and Raegan plan theirs. Now they were all mad and shit.

"Ain't nobody tell you to go trying to one up these niggas." Raegan rolled her eyes as she grabbed a bag of Funyuns off the shelf.

We were making our last pit stop before we entered St. Louis. We didn't want the guys to know that they were stressed about planning our dates. Rae and Hope waited until we were in the gas station to release all their frustrations.

"I don't know what you're so mad about. It's just a date. Hell, you could take him to the damn movies and sneak some Sour Patch Kids in your purse and he would be satisfied." I waved her off.

"Is that what you're planning to do with Zu?" Raegan asked.

I shook my head no.

"Exactly. After the thought and planning that went into that Chicago stop, there ain't no way I can get away with no average bullshit like that."

She was right, but it wasn't my fault. I wanted to do something nice for Zu. He was the one who ran his big mouth to his boys. I wasn't taking the blame for that.

"Don't blame me! Zuvhir is the one who told all our business. But it's really not even that deep."

I grabbed an ice cold Pepsi from the cooler and joined Hope at the front of the store.

"It is that deep, Sage! We have to do something that'll prove that we're just as, if not more, thoughtful than they are. Lord knows I ain't been listening to that nigga. I've been too busy trying to keep from raping that fool," Hope muttered.

"Wait! Ya'll ain't hunched yet?" Raegan's eyes grew wide.

"Nigga, *hunched*?" Hope burst out laughing.

"What you want me to say? Ya'll ain't boned, done the deed, gotten freaky, did the nasty, bumped uglies, or *fucked* yet?"

"Yes, bitch! Anything would have been better than hunched!"

Hope and I fell out laughing and Raegan eventually joined in. We walked up to the counter and handed our items over to the cashier.

"Well, that's interesting. I for sure thought ya'll had had sex already. Me and Zeek did." She stuck her tongue out, mimicking Cardi B.

"Didn't take a rocket scientist to figure that out, lil' nasty. But I'm trying not to be like your hoe ass." Hope rolled her eyes. "You and Zu had sex yet?"

My cheeks flushed in embarrassment. It wasn't like I didn't know that the conversation would eventually go in that direction, but I was ashamed of the fact that we had yet to consummate our relationship. It wasn't for lack of trying. I had been basically handing Zuvhir my kitty on a silver platter, but he had respectfully declined.

"Um, no actually. We are just kind of waiting on the right moment." I pretended to be nonchalant about it.

"What?!" Raegan screeched. "I can't believe I'm friends with such lames. Ya'll better hop on that—*literally*. I mean, hop on that dick and ride it all the way the hell home."

The gas station clerk looked at us with wide eyes.

Raegan shrugged. "What you all in our business for, Mohammed? You probably got ten wives you giving the D to while you over there judging us. Ring us up, man." Raegan tossed a few dollars on the counter and walked out of the store in a huff. I stifled a laugh and looked at the clerk. Eyeing his name tag, I smiled weakly.

"Sorry, Deon. Please excuse my friend. Have a nice day and keep the change."

I tossed a twenty on the counter and Hope and I quickly exited the store. Once we were outside, we cracked up.

"Can't take that feisty bitch nowhere," Hope said between giggles.

We hopped back into the SUV, and Freak, who was now driving, pulled off. Nightfall had come, and Freak and Hope were having a private conversation up in the front seat while Eric Bellinger lightly filled the truck. Zeek was laid out in his seat with Raegan sleep in his lap, and Zu and I were chilling in the back seat. We were attempting to play a game of Never Have I Ever, but apparently Zu had done a little of everything.

"Ok, never have I ever...eaten ass." I giggled.

Zu's head fell back and my mouth flew open.

"Man, I'm glad we're not doing this with shots," Zu admitted.

"Oh my God! You be tossing salads, nigga?" I giggled.

"Don't knock it til you try it, baby."

"Ewwwe. Whatever. Ok, it's your turn."

Zu thought for a few moments. "Never have I ever gotten head in the back seat of a rented black truck while my homies were inside."

I laughed out loud at how specific his statement was.

"Was that a hint?" I wiggled my eyebrows, kind of happy that he had seemingly given me the green light.

"Nah! I just had to get real detailed because apparently a nigga been out here living real reckless." He laughed.

Before he could get another word out, I anxiously leaned over and started unbuckling his belt. He grabbed at my hands but I swatted them away. I was determined to do this shit tonight.

"Yo! What are you doing?" he whispered as he stole a glance at the front seat.

"Trying to make that *I've never* work in your favor. Lift up."

He sat still for a moment, looking at me with wide eyes. I shot him a look that read, *I ain't playing with you, nigga.* And he quickly got the hint. He lifted his ass off the seat and pulled his jeans and boxers down to reveal his semi hard member. Instantly, my mouth watered. I had never seen a penis so pretty. It looked kind of like a Twix candy bar, and I could only imagine that it tasted just as good.

Stroking it softly with my hand, I felt it grow in length and width. He was working with a beautiful monster.

"Yo, you ain't—"

I shut his ass up as soon as I licked the underside of his dick with the flat of my tongue. Starting from the base of his manhood, I trailed my tongue up and used the tip of my tongue to lightly tease the head. He cleared his throat, ready to say something else, but I was tired of talking. Puckering my lips, I slipped his thick rod inside my mouth and took him all the way to the back of my throat with lightning speed, making sure to fold my lips over my teeth on my way down. Zu hissed and his body tensed as I bobbed up and down on his dick, allowing my mouth to get wet with spit. I took my tongue and flattened it against the underside of him once again and continued my bobbing motion.

"Goddamn," Zuvhir groaned.

Hurriedly, Zu yanked off the hair tie that was holding my bun together and tossed it on the floor. Gripping my hair at the root, he pulled at it, now controlling my pace. My mouth leaked like a broken faucet all over him as I continued to deep throat him. I lifted my eyes to see his face, and it contorted in the most beautiful way. His eyes were shut and his brow was furrowed. Zu's top lip was curled up in a snarl and the veins in his neck were popping. The sight of him made my pussy wet and I wanted nothing more than to hop up and straddle his lap. We were already doing the most in the back seat so there was no way we would be able to get away with fucking while our friends were in the car, so I continued to suck him off. I suctioned my lips around him and pulled, popping his manhood out of my mouth like a watermelon Blow Pop before placing him back in my mouth and repeating the process.

"Sage, man...I...I'm 'bout to cum."

He didn't have to tell me. I could feel the change in his body. I took his balls in my hand, tugging on them a little bit and hummed along to "Plush Duvet," which was playing on the car's stereo.

"Mmmmmmmmmm!"

Zuvhir kept his mouth shut, careful not to give away the freak shit we were doing in the back of the car, but he was straining. He wanted to cry out but instead he used one hand to grip the back of my head and the other to clamp down on the back seat cushion. With nowhere to go, I swallowed every drop he'd rained down my throat and was sure to lick him clean. Yeah, I was a good girl with her head on straight, her credit on fleek, and her priorities in check, but I was also a freak for the nigga that went hard for me. And Zu only got a glimpse of what I was a capable of.

Picking myself up off the floor of the truck, I took my seat next to him, wiping at the corners of my mouth. Silence moved between us as Zu struggled to catch his breath and I dug around my purse for a stick of gum. I found my pack of Polar Ice and pulled out a stick and popped it in my mouth. I peeked over at Zuvhir and watched him lazily stuff himself back into his boxers and then pull up his pants. He must've felt me staring, so looked up at me.

"You wild, man." He smirked.

"I got tired of you holding out on me." I shrugged.

Zuvhir positioned himself with his back against the window and his leg propped up on the seat. He pulled at me until I was sitting between his legs with my back facing his chest.

"You different, Sagey. A nigga like me would have been tapped that, but I wanted you to understand that it wasn't just physical between us. I wanted you to know that I recognized that you were special."

"I understand, but I didn't need you to hold out on me in order to prove how you felt about me. I can feel it when you look at me. I knew it when you made me handle my business with Dominick. To be honest, I knew when you tried to protect me from you."

I felt his hands at the top of my hairline and I relaxed into his body. He brushed his fingers lightly across my baby hairs and rested his other hand underneath my shirt right on my stomach.

"I just want this to be different, yo. I wanted to take my time. We got time. We don't have to rush anything."

Tears welled up in my eyes and I was glad that he couldn't see my face.

"We may not have the time you think we do." I whispered.

"What does that mean?" I could feel his body go rigid underneath mine.

"Just...just that tomorrow isn't promised. We never know what's going to happen and while I don't necessarily think we should rush, I think we should take into consideration that the only thing we know for sure is that we have today."

"Sage, what—"

"It's nothing," I said, cutting him off. I'm just talking. I'm glad that you care enough about me to make things special and to make me feel special."

I yawned, hoping that he would catch my drift that this conversation had come to an end for now. I snuggled up under him and rested my head on his chest, the tears falling like snow against my face. Placing my hand under my cheek, I caught them before they could hit his shirt and for some reason, that action only made the tears fall harder. His arms wrapped around me, instantly making me feel safe and warm, even with the air conditioner on full blast thanks to Hope. I prayed a silent prayer before I closed my eyes and nodded off, my secret weighing heavy on my heart.

Chapter Twenty-Seven
Zuvhir

I dropped Sage and my luggage on the floor and took a look at the room we'd rented for the night. We had checked into the Four Seasons and just gotten to our room, which had a dope view of the Gateway Arch. There was a casino right downstairs, and a nigga was itching to hit the tables. But it was Sage's turn to plan something for us to do, so I was going to hang tight and see what she had up her sleeve. She had come in and ran straight to the bathroom to shower, so I went through my bags to find something to match my baby's fly for the night.

While Sagey sang her little heart out in the shower, I got dressed in a pair of heather black Nike joggers, a white tee, and matching heather black zip up hoodie. Sagey had asked me to dress casual, so a nigga was lightweight excited because I knew whatever she had planned was about to be fun. I threw my dreads up on top of my head and switched out my black diamond studs for my white gold pair. Pulling out some Carmex, I squeezed a little on my index finger and smoothed it over my lips. I figured that Sage would probably be a while, I hopped my ready ass onto the bed and turned on the TV. As soon as I settled on ESPN, Sage came bouncing out of the bathroom, dressed and ready to roll. She looked so damn cute dressed down in her baggy black harem joggers and her Ivy Park sports bra. She hit me with a grin when she caught me staring and slid the black pullover hoodie she held in her hands, over her head.

"You ready, bae?" she asked, slipping her feet into a pair of black Huaraches.

"Yup," I said as I hopped up off the bed.

"Wait. First we have to do something." She smirked.

Going into her bag, she produced a bottle of Hennessey Black and a pack of Solo red shot cups.

"Aww, shit! We 'bout to turn up?" I asked.

"Yup. You have five guesses as to where we're going for our date. It's a two part date so for every correct guess, I take a shot. For every wrong guess, you have to take a shot."

Damn, I loved this girl. Most broads would have been trying to hit the city's more expensive restaurant or most exclusive boutiques, but Sage was fun as fuck. She genuinely enjoyed being with a nigga and she'd put effort into making our time together fun and different. I dug that shit.

"Bet, baby. You on. A'ight. My first guess is that we're going to get some food. We ain't had nothing to eat in five hours, so I know that's gotta be on the list," I said confidently.

"You gotta be specific!" she laughed.

"Nah, nah. Don't be adding rules and shit. Run that shot, lil' mama."

She giggled and waved me off. After blessing the bottle, Sage poured herself a shot and took it to the head, no chaser. Baby girl was a G.

"Ok, second guess."

"A'ight, uh… We going to some Dave and Busters type shit," I guessed.

"Nnnnkkk! Wrong! Drink up, Zu!"

Sage poured me a shot and handed it over. I tossed it back with ease and tried my hand at guessing again. Man, a nigga got all the rest of my guesses wrong! I was four shots deep by the time we got in the Uber, but it was all good. I wasn't a lightweight by any means. Sage allowed me to continue to guess if I agreed to drink after every wrong guess, so by the time the driver pulled up to our destination, a nigga was good and tipsy. I made sure that Sage got a few more in her too so she was near my level once we hopped out of the car.

"Where we at boo?" I asked, looking around in the dark trying to figure out where the hell we had been dropped off at.

Suddenly, a beam of light streamed ahead of us, and I saw a large graffiti wall. I turned toward where the light had come from and saw Sage standing there pointing a flashlight in the direction of the wall with a devilish grin on her face.

"Sage, what the—"

The rattle of a spray can made me look down at Sage's hand, and sure enough she had a bottle of spray paint in her now gloved hands.

"Are you serious right now, girl? We could get arrested for this shit!"

"Aw, don't tell me that the retired kingpin is afraid of a little law enforcement," she mocked.

Not waiting for me to say anything else, she tossed me a can of spray paint and jogged over to me.

"C'mon, scary cat. Show me what you got."

Without another word, Sage took off toward the wall, looking for a spot to tag. She surprised me more and more every day. Not only was she a little rebel, but she could also do graffiti. I watched in awe as she tagged a small space on the wall with red, pink, and white spray paint. She wrote 'Sage and Zu' in 3-D bubble letters with small animated hearts flying around it. Shit was girly but dope. I didn't know that Sage had that kind of skill.

"Let me find out that you were a little thug in a past life." I laughed as she finished up.

"I'll never tell." She laughed. "Your turn."

"A'ight, but you can't see it until I'm finished."

She pouted, but I didn't start until she agreed and turned her back to the wall. Finding a space to start, a nigga went in. The idea just came to me, and the art just flowed. There was no thought process to this piece. It was just a mirror of what a nigga was feeling. Twenty minutes in and Sage started getting impatient.

"Are you done?" she whined.

"Yes, cry baby. You can turn around." I dropped the last of the spray cans on the ground and let out a deep breath.

A gasp flew out of Sage's mouth, and it caused me to step back and take a look at my work. It was a picture of Sage's hands, identifiable by the small Roman numeral tattoo on her left middle finger and the ring the always wore on her right ring finger. They were holding a heart. The heart was an anatomical one, and it looked as if it were beating. The veins had been drawn to spell out my name. I was more proud of this piece than anything I'd ever drawn or painted in my life. It had been years since I had picked up a pencil, paint brush, or spray can, but when I did, everything just flowed effortlessly. This girl just had that effect on me.

"Baby, it's beautiful," she whispered.

"Come here."

Sage trotted over to me, and I held her in my arms. I was about to say some real sentimental shit to her, but I was interrupted by police sirens. We pulled away from each other and turned toward the sirens to see two police cars on their way toward us.

"Shit! Fucking with your thug ass!" I yelled. "Run baby! Go!"

Sage and I took off running in the opposite direction as the sirens got closer and closer to us. I turned around to survey how close the cops were and heard Sage laughing hysterically. We ducked under an underpass and ran up the hill onto a street, where we slowed our pace and blended into the crowd. Once we rounded the corner, I grabbed Sage's ass up and pulled her into a small alley, pinning her against the wall. Her eyes grew big, and I could feel her heart beating like a drum cadence against her chest. Gripping her waist, I leaned in and kissed her passionately. She returned the kiss with angst, her hands finding their way to my neck, pulling my face closer to hers. I ran my hands up her back, catching some of her sweat on the way and let my tongue dance inside her mouth as my lips tangoed with hers. I pulled away after a few moments, and we just stared at each other until we both burst out laughing.

"Yo, you fucking wild, man." I laughed.

"You love it, though." Sage pecked at my lips and walked back onto the street.

I shook my head and followed her. Wasn't shit a nigga could say. She was right. I loved every fucking thing about my baby.

Chapter Twenty-Eight
Sage

I was laughing so hard that I was getting light-headed. We were in an Uber car on our way to our final destination and my personal favorite, Hotlanta. Raegan and Zeek were filling us in on their date night, and it was a hilarious hot ass mess.

"Then she dragged me to some shit called painting with a twist. First of all, do I look like a nigga that even knows how to hold a damn paintbrush?"

Hope and I howled at the mug that Zeek wore on his face. Raegan had her face all frowned up and her arms firmly folded across her chest, mad at the world.

"The instructor came in dressed like one of the children of the corn and talkin' 'bout us painting a damn vase of flowers. The fuck? Then the broad gets all excited about *the twist*. I go to ask Rae what that means, and she tells me we get to drink. So I'm thinking ok, cool. At least I can get drunk during this shit."

Zeek looked over at Rae with an irritated scowl, and Rae rolled her eyes hard, before she turned and faced the window.

"*Mannn*, the Amish bitch teaching the class disappeared and came back with three damn bottles of THOT juice."

Zu busted out laughing. "What the fuck is THOT juice, bruh?"

"Some damn flavored Moscato!"

A chorus of 'aww mans' floated through the car from the guys, and Hope and I grabbed onto each other as we laughed.

"It ain't that damn funny!" Rae snapped.

"Yes, the hell it is. Why in the hell would you think that man wanted to paint, Rae?" Hope asked between laughs.

Raegan pouted. "I told ya'll I wasn't good at that shit."

"It's ok, my baby more than made up for it last night under them sheets! Showed me alll the thangs that mouf can do!" Zeek screamed.

Zu and Freak dapped Zeek up while Rae shoved the shit out of him.

"Don't be putting all my business out in the streets like that, nigga!"

"Chill, man. These your homies and my niggas."

Zeek rolled down the window and shouted out: "Rae's a stone cold freak, though!" Turning back to an astonished Rae, he smirked.

"Now, if I had done some shit like that, you would be mad."

We laughed for another few minutes at Rae and Zeek's crazy asses before night started to fall and everyone started getting sleepy. My head was banging so I reached around in my purse for a pill and popped it. Twenty minutes later, your girl was knocked out.

We finally arrived in Atlanta later and pulled up at the Mandarin Oriental Hotel. The hotel was gorgeous, looking more like a modern-day castle than a hotel, and I was floored by the elegant décor throughout the lobby. I snapped a few pictures on my phone for my vision board before we made our way up to the room. Zuvhir had booked us the Mandarin Suite which featured a full dining room, beautiful high ceilings, two large balconies with sprawling views of the city, and a master bathroom laid in marble. The bed was draped in a powder blue velvet canopy and backed by a tufted headboard of the same fabric. The cool blues, beige, and browns made the room sophisticated and modern, and I instantly fell in love.

"Oh my God! This place is beautiful. One of the most beautifully decorated hotel rooms I've ever stayed in."

Zuvhir came up behind me and wrapped his hands around my waist, nuzzling his face with mine.

"I know. I picked out all the hotels because of their décor. I wanted it to inspire you."

Love rushed through my body, and I could say without a doubt that I felt full. Little things like this made me ecstatic that I listened to my first mind and continued to pursue Zu even though he kept pushing me away. He knew my heart, and that was amazing because we hadn't known each other that long.

"I love you." I smiled, feeling happier than I ever remembered feeling.

Zuvhir kissed my neck softly. "I love you too." He pulled away and smacked me on the ass. "Now, go get ready."

We were all going to hang out tonight, and I was glad. I had a ton of fun with Zeek and Freak and of course with Hope and Sage. It was dope that my group of friends had been able to connect with his, and I hoped their connections were as strong as Zu's and mine. I grabbed my bag and headed to the bathroom to get ready for the night. I popped a handful of my prescription pills in my mouth and washed them down with a bottle of water. After pinning my hair up and throwing on a shower cap, I stepped into the shower and started the process.

Once I was done in the bathroom, I walked out to find a garment bag draped over one of the living room chairs with a note attached. I walked toward it as I dried myself off and grabbed the note up.

Bought you a little something to wear tonight. Hope you like it. Meet me in the bar in an hour. –Zu

Grinning, I unzipped the bag and was super excited at what I saw. Inside was an olive green, basket weaved, wrap pencil skirt and a crème strapless crop top with an attached choker. In the seat of the chair was a box of shoes. I opened it and was greeted by a pair of gold snakeskin Brian Atwood strappy sandals. There was another small box, which I opened to reveal a gold clutch, a pair of thin gold hoops, and a few gold rings. Completely satisfied with the outfit that Zu had purchased for me, I moisturized myself down with lotion and sprayed my Tom Ford Orchid Soleil perfume in all the right places before I started to get dressed. Forty minutes later, I stood in front of the full-length mirror, beaming. I had flat ironed my hair bone straight and was rocking it with a deep side part. My makeup was dewy and golden, completed by a metallic matte brownish-gold lipstick. I looked stunning and I thought everyone would agree. Love looked good on me.

Chapter Twenty Nine
Zuvhir

"Damn, that shit was turnt!" Freak wiped the sweat from under his snapback before placing it back on his head.

My nigga wasn't lying. After having dinner at one of the hotel's restaurants, we had caught an Uber SUV over to Compound, a popular ATL night club, and fucking lived life. We secured a VIP section and a few bottles and parlayed with the big dawgs. Sage had wanted to enjoy the weather so we copped us a little section outside alongside some of Atlanta's black IT crowd. TI and Tiny were in the booth to our left and Young Jeezy and Trey Songz were in the booth across from us. The girls nearly lost their shit.

"Baby!" Sage's drunk ass strutted over to me with her eyes low.

I wrapped her up in my arms and stole a kiss. My baby was a showstopper tonight, looking better than all the celebrity chicks in attendance. I knew half the club was wondering who the hell we were. A group of well-dressed niggas with three of the baddest women in the state, blowing bands, was definitely going to attract some attention, so I already knew what it was.

"What we about to do now?" Sage asked, her face buried in my chest as my hands roamed her ass.

"I'm bout to take your drunk ass to the hotel and get you in bed."

Sage pulled away from me, staring at me with sultry eyes.

"And then?"

"And then I'ma give your ass some water and aspirin so that you won't be throwing up all over that expensive-ass fit I bought you." I laughed.

"Zuuuuuu!" she whined.

I watched her mouth form into a pout and laughed. She was feenin' for the dick. Although I had really wanted to wait for a perfect moment, our epic-ass trip was coming to an end and hitting her off now would probably be a good way to end our adventure.

I pulled her closed and positioned my mouth near her ear. "You want this dick, huh?"

"Yessss," she whined again.

"Tell me you want this dick then, girl."

Surprising the shit out of me, Sage eased her hand down my stomach and to the front of my jeans, grabbing my package gently with her hand.

"I want you to put this big, thick, dick inside this hot, wet pussy...*your* hot, wet pussy," she moaned.

Instantly, I rocked up right in her hands. I had a little freak on my hands. Now more anxious than ever to get back to the room, I removed her fingers from around me and signaled for our friends to come the fuck on. We called an Uber and made it back to the hotel in no time. Sage and I hurriedly said our goodbyes and headed for the elevator, while the group stayed back trying to decide on whether or not they were going to grab some food from Waffle House. Once Sage and I were in the elevator, she pounced on a nigga like a cheetah.

Her hands were up my shirt, and her fingers grazed my skin as our lips met. I ran my fingers through her silky hair as I tongued her down, tasting the Hennessey she had drank and the mint that still lingered in her mouth. The elevator dinged, signaling we were on our floor, and we tumbled out, still tangled up in each other. Without breaking our kiss we made it to our door and I pinned her against it, holding her arms at her wrists above her head. I made a trail of kisses from her lips to her breasts, eliciting a soft moan from her. Taking my free hand, I pulled down her strapless top, freeing her pretty brown breasts dotted with chocolate nipples. My mouth salivated at the sight, and a nigga had to go in for a taste. Latching on to the right nipple, I drew circles around her areola while I held the nipple between my teeth. She inhaled sharply and tried to wiggle free from my grasp. I tightened my grip and continued to play with her pretty titties while my free hand found its way inside her skirt. I could feel a slight raise in the skin underneath her left breasts and curiosity got the best of me. I stopped my tongue action to get a better look at what my fingers had felt but Sage stopped me. She moved my hands from her breast to the top of her ass and smashed her lips against mine. A nigga was so horny that whatever I was thinking about before she'd kissed me, was now null and void. My fingers had a mind of their own as they crawled down her lower back and eased into the crack of her plump ass.

"Zuuu...," Sage said on a soft breath.

I bit down gently on her nipple, and she hissed like a rattlesnake. I used the hand that was roaming her ass to push her body closer to mine. Letting go of her nipple, I let my face rest between her breasts, breathing in her scent. Then I licked a trail from the top of her cleavage to the underside of her left breast until I got to the neglected nipple. The elevator dinged behind us, letting us know that we were about to have a spectator, but I didn't give a fuck.

"Somebody's coming," she moaned.

As much as I didn't give a fuck, I didn't want Sage out in the hallway ass naked for the world to see, so I quickly pulled out the key card, inserted it into the door lock and opened it. Sage and I tumbled inside and fell to the floor right next to each other as the door slammed shut. Our laughter filled the room for a few moments, followed by deep breathing. I rolled over so that I could look my baby in the eyes. Sage turned and did the same. We stared at each other, the heat of the moment rising until it bubbled over and we attacked each other all over again.

I rolled over on top of Sage, hungrily kissing her lips and hugging her close to my body. Her finger lazily dragged up my back as she tried to open her legs to allow my body to fit between them. Her skirt was constricting, so I pulled away and flipped her over on her stomach roughly and unzipped the skirt. I eased it off her body, not taking my eyes off her bare ass. My lil' freak hadn't even worn underwear tonight. I bit my lip and shook my head. Once her skirt was flung across the room, I parted her ass cheeks and dove in. She shrieked in delight as my tongue produced long, wet licks inside her ass crack, stopping to play with her forbidden hole. She might have been a freak, but I was a nasty nigga.

Needing more access, I lifted her lower body up so that she was bent over on her knees and her pretty round brown ass was primed for this tongue action I was about to whip on her. Taking my pointed tongue from the top of her ass and dragging it all the way down to her pretty, freshly shaved pussy, I licked her up like my favorite ice cream.

"Goddamnnn, Zuuuuuuu!" she sang.

Her screams were like music to my ears. I buried my face between her ass cheeks and gave them a slap. Her meaty flesh jiggled around me and I inhaled her feminine scent. Eagerly, I attacked her pussy with my lips and tongue, determined to make my baby squirt. She was bucking against my stiff tongue and rotating her hips making sure I hit every nook and cranny. A nigga wasn't mad.

"Shit! Baby, I'm about to…"

I pulled myself away from her, pausing right before she was about to let loose. She whipped her head around like the goddamn crazy chick on Exorcist, but before she could speak, I assaulted her pussy with a vibrating tongue and twisted my index finger inside of her while my thumb stroked her clit all at the same damn time.

"Zu, baby, I'm cummiiing!"

224

Sage's juices sprayed out like a broken fire hydrant. Not wanting to waste a drop, I kept my mouth on her until she had released it all. Weak with pleasure, Sage collapsed on the floor as I laughed. I let her recoup as I went the bathroom to grab a towel to clean off my face. When I returned, I came up out of my clothes and reached out to Sage to help her off the floor.

"Mmm... I'm tired," she replied woozily.

"Nah, you wanted this dick, remember? You 'bout to ride this muh'fucka."

I dragged her over to the bed where she took a seat on the edge. Feeling like the room had gotten a little stuffy, I ran over to open the balcony doors, and cool air rushed in. I made my way back to the bed and hopped up.

"C'mon, Sagey. Come get what you've been begging a nigga for," I said lowly as I stroked myself.

Sage crawled toward me until she was near my lap, and then lifted herself up and straddled me. She knocked my hand away from my dick, licking her lips in anticipation. She positioned it right at her opening. Slowly and torturously, she used the tip of my dick to stroke her clit, throwing her head back in pleasure.

"Stop playing with a nigga and get up here," I growled.

Smirking, she positioned my thick pole and slowly slid down on it, allowing her pussy to adjust to the width of me. It took her a few moments, but once I was finally all the way in, we released moans simultaneously. A nigga had been up in some pussy before, but Sage was so fucking warm and wet, a nigga felt like that white dude on American Pie.

"Zu, fuck!"

She hadn't even started moving yet and she was already feeling it. I slapped her on the ass to get her motivated, and she started to bounce. Up and down, up and down, her pussy did hydraulics on my dick. Her walls conformed to the curve of me, and I felt myself slipping into her quicksand. I bit my lip, trying to control the bitch-ass moan that was about to escape, but I'll be damned if it didn't slip out anyway. Grabbing her titties in my hands, I massaged them as Sage did her thang, grinding and twerking all over my lap. My fingers landed on that same raised spot I had found earlier and I found myself lingering there longer than normal, trying to figure out what the fuck it was. I don't know if I was tripping but it felt like as soon as I found that spot again, Sage started bouncing harder and faster, causing my attention to wane away from the raised skin.

"Deeper!" she screamed.

And just like that, her wish was my command. I lifted my hips off the bed and thrust into her gently at first and after I felt myself break into a new level of her wet tunnel, a nigga couldn't control the speed. Letting her breasts go, I grabbed at her wide hips and slammed her body onto mine as I plunged deeper inside her. "Damn, Sagey. You so fucking wet, Ma. You wet for me baby? I made that pussy super-soaker wet?" I asked.

"Yes, baby. Yes!" Sage moaned with her eyes closed.

"Open them eyes. Let me look at you," I demanded.

She opened them, and our eyes locked, and I felt like my dick stretched an extra three inches. Just looking into her sultry brown eyes and seeing the love and lust radiate from them had me gone. I brought her body forward and sucked on her neck like I needed her blood to live. My lower body was going ape off in that thang, and her screams bounced off the wall like dodge balls.

"Zuvhirrrrrrrrrrrr! I fucking love you!" she squealed.

I think I whispered I love you too, but I honestly couldn't tell you. I went outside of my mind as I tried to fuck Sagey into another stratosphere.

"I'm commmmmmmmminnnnnnngggggggg!"

Sage's walls tightened around me and then I felt a rush of liquid love rain down on me. It was a wrap for a nigga. I felt Sage go limp in my arms, and I released all my lil' niggas inside her. Breathing hard, I sank into the bed, trying to get myself together as Sage laid across my chest.

After a few minutes, I chuckled and tapped Sage on her ass. "A'ight, girl. You gotta get up. You heavy."

She didn't move, which caused another chuckle to fall from my lips. I knew she was exhausted, but she was going to have to get over it because we were definitely going another round. I tapped her again.

"Sagey, baby. Get up."

When she didn't move this time, my heart leapt out of my chest. Gently pushing her off my chest, I looked down at her for the first time. Her eyes were closed and her mouth was open, but her chest wasn't rising and falling. I grabbed her wrist to feel for a pulse while trying to keep my cool. When I didn't feel one, I fucking lost it.

"Sage! *Saaaage!*"

TO BE CONTINUED...

OTHER BOOKS BY BRI NOREEN:

Long As You Know Who You Belong To
Long As You Know Who You Belong To 2
Long As You Know Who You Belong To 3
The Royal Family

CPSIA information can be obtained
at www.ICGtesting.com
Printed in the USA
LVOW10s1733271016
510551LV00013B/1531/P